WHISKEY REVEALS

CARRIE ANN RYAN

Whiskey Reveals

A Whiskey and Lies Novel

By: Carrie Ann Ryan

ISBN: 978-1-943123-86-5

Cover Art by Charity Hendry

Photo by Jenn Leblanc

For more information, please join Carrie Ann's MAILING LIST.

To interact with Carrie Ann Ryan, you can join her FAN CLUB.

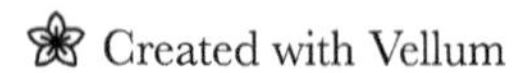

Praise for Carrie Ann Ryan....

"Carrie Ann Ryan knows how to pull your heartstrings and make your pulse pound! Her wonderful Redwood Pack series will draw you in and keep you reading long into the night. I can't wait to see what comes next with the new generation, the Talons. Keep them coming, Carrie Ann!"

–Lara Adrian, New York Times bestselling author of CRAVE THE NIGHT

"Carrie Ann Ryan never fails to draw readers in with passion, raw sensuality, and characters that pop off the page. Any book by Carrie Ann is an absolute treat."

–New York Times Bestselling Author J. Kenn

"With snarky humor, sizzling love scenes, and br
imaginative worldbuilding, The Dante's Circle series
if Carrie Ann Ryan peeked at my personal wish lis

–NYT Bestselling Author, Larissa Ione

"Carrie Ann Ryan writes sexy shifters in a world full of passionate happily-ever-afters."

–*New York Times* Bestselling Author Vivian Arend

"Carrie Ann's books are sexy with characters you can't help but love from page one. They are heat and heart blended to perfection."

–*New York Times* Bestselling Author Jayne Rylon

Carrie Ann Ryan's books are wickedly funny and deliciously hot, with plenty of twists to keep you guessing. They'll keep you up all night!"

–USA Today Bestselling Author Cari Quinn

"Once again, Carrie Ann Ryan knocks the Dante's Circle series out of the park. The queen of hot, sexy, enthralling paranormal romance, Carrie Ann is an author not to miss!"

–*New York Times* bestselling Author Marie Harte

Dedication

To the whiskey lovers who happen to love Whiskey and Lies.
This one is for you.

Whiskey Reveals

One whiskey-saturated night turns into something far more in the second standalone installment of the bestselling Whiskey and Lies series from NYT Bestselling Author Carrie Ann Ryan.

Fox Collins likes his life just the way it is. His siblings are falling in love all around him, but he'd much rather focus on his next story than on a serious relationship. However, when his latest one-night stand returns to Whiskey—this time for good—he'll need to learn to trust his instincts to figure out if he can live without her in his life.

Former dancer Melody Waters is finally ready to settle down in her grandmother's small Pennsylvania hometown. Bad decisions and fateful nights have changed her path more than once, but now she's focused on one thing: opening her new own dance studio. But fate is a funny thing, and once again, she'll be forced to learn that actions have consequences and some repercussions can not only change your life forever, they can also come back to haunt you…one broken promise at a time.

Chapter 1

Fox Collins never wanted to wake up.

At least not while he was having the best damn dream of his life. He wasn't necessarily fully asleep at the moment, but rather half dream-like snoozing, where he could wield his subconscious to finish the delicious dream he'd been having. Meaning, any sound could wake him up, and thinking about it too hard could also rip him from sleep.

That meant he quickly shoved those too complicated thoughts out of his head to avoid waking and went back to the delectable blonde currently sucking his cock. Sadly, she was only his dream woman, not real, but he'd take what he could get since this was one damn sexy figment of his imagination. The fact that she was sort of based on a real person was, again, one of those thoughts he wasn't going to think about since he wanted this part of his morning to continue.

His blonde licked up his shaft, her tongue like magic and warmth and everything that made him want to come right there. But he held himself back—barely. She slowly sucked on the crown, the tip of her tongue playing with his slit, and his eyes mentally rolled to the back of his head, his body shaking both in and out of the dream.

She was so damn sexy, all curves and softness. There was a strength to her, as well. Something that had taken him for a ride the one time they'd had sex out of his dreams, but he wasn't going to focus on that either. Instead, he would only think about her on her knees on the bed in front of him, as he lay back to let her suck him down. She bobbed her head, her eyes meeting his as she took him whole.

He didn't reach out to touch her, didn't let his hands follow the curves of her soft skin. As soon as he did that, he knew he'd wake up. He always did. Because he'd never be able to reach her. It was as if his brain wouldn't allow him to remember exactly how perfect she felt in his arms—even if those memories were wrapped in a whiskey-laced fog.

His blonde squeezed his dick, and his eyes crossed, his hips bucking off the bed. He shouted her name, but only her first since she'd refused to give him her last, and found himself awake in his bed, his stomach sticky, and his own hand wrapped around the base of his cock.

He was alone, somewhat sated, and as he looked over at the clock on his nightstand…running late.

"Well, Melody, it seems I just can't quit you." His voice sounded loud in the emptiness of his room, and he let out a sigh. Apparently, Fox wasn't the best at one-night stands—even if he'd tried to be. And, now, the blonde from his single night playing with whiskey and fate haunted his dreams and his dick.

He quirked a smile at that. A haunted dick? That could

be a fun story to write. He might be the owner and editor of the *Whiskey Chronicles*, but he could take an afternoon and write a short story just for fun. It would keep his skills sharp, and frankly, he could use a laugh. It had been a long few months with deadline after deadline, and his dream woman continued to seep into his subconscious to the point where he wasn't sleeping nearly enough.

His second alarm went off on his phone, and he sighed. He'd jacked off in his sleep through the first one, and that meant he had no more time to stay wrapped in his sweaty sheets and brood. Plus, he wasn't the broody brother, he let that title go to Loch—and maybe even Dare before he'd met Kenzie.

And now, he was thinking about his brothers and his future sister-in-law while naked in bed because he didn't want to get up and go to work.

He'd officially hit rock bottom.

Fox rolled out of bed, careful to keep his dick close to his stomach so he didn't make more of a mess and went to clean himself up at least slightly. Before he even took a shower, he went back into his bedroom and stripped off his sheets. This was the second time this week he'd woken to a dream like that, and he was already getting tired of doing laundry.

Knowing he needed coffee before he did anything else, he strode naked to his kitchen and made himself a cup while checking his email and looking over the news on his phone. He'd read the physical publications as well since he was in the paper business and tried to keep up with both formats, but for now, he just wanted to check on any headlines. And with the world as it was, it seemed there was almost hourly breaking news these days.

That was one reason he liked living and working in Whiskey. It was not only his hometown where he knew every single person in residence—other than the tourists, of course—but it was also quiet enough most days that he could get to the heart of the town with its news rather than reading horror stories day in and day out. Maybe, at one time in his life, he'd have liked to be the hardcore reporter who worked on terrifying and heartbreaking news until the wee hours of the morning, but he'd learned long ago that he needed balance in his life in order to make his writing mean something. There needed to be substantial pieces of good news amongst the horrors, and finding a way to do that without looking as if they were merely fluff pieces was his juggling act.

"And now I'm getting *way* too philosophical on half a cup of coffee. Not to mention, talking to myself." He drained the rest of his mug and set it under the spout for when he got out of the shower and wanted his second cup. He was on a three-cup-a-day rule and would switch to water after his third, but he tended to drink all three at once. Probably not exactly what his doctor wanted, but it wasn't as if he were going to change his habits anytime soon.

Fox rolled his shoulders and, still naked, made his way back the bathroom so he could shower and finish getting ready for the day. For a man already late, he sure was taking his time. Of course, since he owned the paper, he could come and go as he pleased, but he didn't like showing up after the rest of his staff. He needed to at least show *some* responsibility.

Thoughts of his dream blonde filtered into his mind again, and his cock stiffened once more. Defeated, he looked down at his stiffening dick and frowned.

"Traitor."

He didn't live by his dick and actually needed to get to work, so it looked as though he'd be finishing up his shower as a cold one. Again.

Damn it.

Chapter 2

"I have eleven inches of copy, but I need to cut it down to ten," Nancy, his sports writer, said as she frowned down at her work. "They're a damn good eleven."

Fox resisted rolling his eyes since this wasn't the first time Nancy had come into his office wanting more space for her work. He kept his gaze on the balls in front of him, juggling so he could keep his mind on task rather than floating to the million and one things he needed to get done before they got the paper out in the morning, as well as the countless stories that needed to be done during the week for the online editions.

"I'm sure they're good. But you have room for ten inches, so cut." He set one ball down on his desk and caught the other two in one hand. It had taken him years to get that trick down, but he couldn't smile in victory while being the boss. He didn't usually juggle while his reporters were talking to him, but Nancy had come into his office unannounced, and he hadn't bothered to stop what he was doing. When he needed to think about his work and couldn't get in the right mindset, he juggled, and Nancy had interrupted that. Again. But this was his job, so he didn't grumble like he might have otherwise.

"But I have eleven." She raised her chin, and he held back a sigh. "At least read it and tell me what you think."

He nodded. "Send it over." In all honesty, the eleven inches were probably better than great, but he didn't have space for that extra inch. They'd make it work if needed, but that wasn't the point.

Nancy beamed. "Thank you." She pressed something on her tablet, and his computer beeped, signaling an email. "I'll be out there working on my next story." She gave him a nod before leaving him alone in his office. Thankfully, she shut the door behind her so he could get his thoughts in order.

He had two large pieces he was currently working on that would take a couple of days to get done, plus an upcoming editorial that he'd been looking forward to for the past few months. He needed to get his interviews scheduled, look over the next set of stories coming in, and do a few more admin things before he headed out for the day, but he was getting things done—even if he was still exhausted from not sleeping well enough. He could blame his imaginary blonde all he wanted, but he knew it wasn't only her. Not this time. He was the one dreaming of her, after all. He needed to get her out of his head and away from his dreams.

He'd met her once at his brother's bar. Had *far* too much whiskey, and had taken her home where he'd proceeded to have the best sex of his life. She'd been gone the next morning with just a note saying "thank you." That was it. No number, no promises, just the memory of her taste and her torn panties on his floor.

Of course, now, he was thinking of the fact that she'd left his house in a dress wearing no panties, and he had to force himself to think of hockey stats so he could keep his erection under control. He was at work for hell's sake.

He looked down at the time on his computer and shook his head. He wasn't getting work done in his office today, so he'd just take his work to his brother's place and get the buzz of tourists and the town into his system. If anyone from the office needed him, they knew how to get ahold of him and where to find him. Most of them worked outside the office a couple of times a week since sitting in one place for too long wasn't always conducive to writing.

He let the others know where he was going, packed up his laptop, tablet, and the other things he needed to get his work done, and headed down the street to the Old Whiskey Bar and Resturant with the Old Whiskey Inn attached to the top levels. He didn't know how his brother handled all of that on his own. Well, he *did* since Kenzie managed the inn, and Dare had a whole staff for the restaurant side, but in the end, Dare did most of the work, especially after their parents retired. More often than not, Fox came in and helped out behind the bar on the weekends since that's what family did, but Dare could have done it without him. His former cop brother was that capable and more. And now that he had Kenzie in his life, Fox had a feeling Dare would get even better at managing all aspects of his life.

Hell, he already handled being a father and working the hours he did. And their other brother, Loch, did the same with his daughter, Misty—and Loch didn't even have the girl's mother in the picture like Dare did with Nate's mom.

Their sister, Tabby, was a newlywed out in Denver and managed a whole company as well as her husband Alex's photography career since she was just that damn good at scheduling. Somehow, Fox felt like the slacker of the bunch without kids and with only one job, but he worked really long hours.

Maybe Fox needed a new hobby or something to make sure he kept up with his siblings. Then he remembered that he was *already* taking night classes for such a thing *and* owned the *Whiskey Chronicles*. He was doing just fine, damn it, and he needed to stop forgetting that. Fox ran a hand over his face, thinking it might not be too early for a drink. Of course, the thought of the last time he'd had a glass of whiskey entered his mind, and he quickly shut it away. No use getting hard and annoyed in front of his family.

Fox passed the hostess station at the bar and nodded at Claire, Dare's front of house manager, as he walked into the building. She smiled, and Fox couldn't help but smile back. Her crisp, white shirt just set off the glow of her dark skin, and every time he came by for dinner, she always took care of him herself. There was no attraction between them, but they were friends who cared about his brother. Out of the corner of his eye, he saw Kenzie moving fast on her sky-high heels as she went up the stairs. Since the inn was on top of the bar and restaurant, she was forever moving from level to level, and because she seemed to be in work mode—something he needed to get into soon—he didn't bother her.

Dare was behind the counter, cleaning glasses like any good barkeep when Fox made his way to the left side of the building where the bar was. Each half of the restaurant served food and drinks, but Fox tended to like the left more since it wasn't as formal and he could hang out with his family. Plus, the other side wasn't open yet since he was here during that weird time between lunch and dinner when the restaurant was setting up for the latter.

"Hey, I thought you were supposed to be working." Dare moved to the soda nozzle and looked up at him. "Though you're probably working here, right?" Fox nodded. "So, no booze. Soda water, or are we going heavy today with something with lots of sugar and caffeine?"

Fox grinned and took a seat on the barstool in front of him. "Soda water with lime. It's not *that* bad of a day." And it really wasn't. He'd just been forced to do a lot of admin work and other things that weren't on his plate when he'd just been a reporter. Being the *owner* of the paper was a far different matter than just working at one, and as each day, month, and year passed, he discovered that fact more and more.

"Well, then, one soda water with lime coming up." Dare slid the glass down the bar like in the old movies their mom had made them watch, and Fox caught it, thankful that his reflexes were sharp. He'd never have lived it down if he missed. Loch and Dare were the more athletic of the four siblings with Tabby now running a close third with her boxing lessons from her husband. Fox could hold his own, but he was still the guy with his head in his books and the clouds most days. He didn't mind, but he also couldn't be the one to break a glass in Dare's bar. He had principles, after all.

"Thanks." Fox saluted with his glass and took a sip. It wasn't his favorite drink in the world, but he'd done his best to cut out excess caffeine and sugar from his day. He wasn't going to count those three cups of coffee as excess.

"So, what are you working on?" Dare went back to cleaning and going through front inventory since it was the slow time of the day, and Fox and another couple were the only ones in the bar.

"A few admin things to get out of the way, but the copy's ready to go for tomorrow. After that, I finally get to get a few notes down for my next project." He couldn't help but grin at that. He'd been waiting to get this interview and piece down since he'd first thought about it for his small town, and though it wouldn't be breaking news or something that would change the world, the person involved *had* changed Whiskey's world with her mere presence. And for that, he was excited.

Dare's eyes lit up. "You finally getting to know Ms. Pearl?"

Fox nodded. "Yep. It's about time Whiskey gets to know their Ms. Pearl."

Ms. Pearl was practically a historical figure in their already historical town. Local legend said that before she settled down in Whiskey, Pennsylvania, she had been a showgirl in Vegas. She had been friends—or at least acquaintances—with the Rat Pack, and Fox was pretty sure she had even more stories to tell. Whiskey had been formed under prohibition law and had the tourist tales to show for it. When Ms. Pearl showed up, she had blended right in with the culture. Of course, when it came to Ms. Pearl, there was nothing *blended* about her. He didn't know if all the stories he'd been told over the years were true, but he was finally getting his chance to hear it from the woman herself. He didn't always get to write editorials about key figures in the town that was part of his soul, but now he would be able to do something he'd always wanted to do. No, it wouldn't change the world but maybe, just maybe, it could change Whiskey.

"Sounds like you have your hands full with Ms. Pearl." Dare grinned and went to take an order from someone who'd come up to the bar. Fox hadn't been there that long, and it was already starting to pick up in business. There was never really any downtime when it came to food and drinks in his town.

Instead of getting distracted by the comings and goings of those around him, he took another sip of his water and opened his computer so he could finish up his admin work for the day. He still needed to read the eleven inches of words from Nancy, and he had a feeling once he got through them, he was going to have to call his department and see what they could do about that extra inch. It wasn't anything new when it came to a small-town paper, but it did make for a headache after a long day of not writing.

He knew he would probably get at least an hour of work done while Dare scurried around him. Kenzie would end up sitting beside Fox at the bar, and then he wouldn't be able to get much work done at all. His future sister-in-law always took his attention because he liked talking with her. But he didn't mind. The two of them had become friends, and he liked that Kenzie was in his life, too. She had changed his brother's world, and for that, he would be forever grateful.

And now that he thought about what day it was, his parents would probably show up soon to catch a bite to eat, too. They had at least one meal a month at his folks' house where it was a huge get-together with plenty of food, lots of talking, and just good people. But ever since the couple had retired, they had taken to eating at either the bar or the restaurant once a week. Considering that they used to work at the same building Dare now owned, Fox knew it probably had more to do with family rather than what they ate that kept them coming back every week. Of course, the food was really good, too.

Since his parents would most likely be there for dinner soon, that meant Loch would probably show up with his daughter, as well. And where his daughter went, Loch's best friend Ainsley usually wasn't far behind.

All of this meant that Fox really needed to focus for the next hour to get as much work done as possible until the horde arrived. Once he headed home after the casual festivities, he'd be able to work some more. He didn't work a nine-to-five job, and he didn't mind. But, sometimes, he thought it would be nice not to bring work home. Of course, he didn't actually know of a job like that, but it was always nice to dream.

He was only twenty minutes into his work when he noticed someone he never thought to see again out of the corner of his eye. He turned, his gaze caught, and his attention enthralled with the woman picking up a to-go order.

Her long, blond hair fell in waves, and she wore tight-fitting jeans that showcased her luscious curves. She had on an elbow-length T-shirt that was tight around her chest and made him remember exactly what she looked like beneath those clothes. He'd tasted every inch of her, touched every curve. It had been in a whiskey-filled haze but he hadn't minded one bit. He could still remember every single instant. Including the fact that she had left him alone in bed the next morning.

"Melody." The word was out of his mouth and echoing in the loud room before he even knew he'd said it.

She turned, her eyes widening for a moment before she schooled her features into a pleasant smile.

"Fox. I should've known I'd see you at this bar again." She held her to-go bag in one hand, and Fox pointedly ignored his brother giving him a look.

"I come here often. My brother is the owner. Remember?"

She gave him another of those sweet smiles that looked nothing like the sultry ones she had given him that night. "Sure I do. Well, it was nice to see you, Fox. As you can see, I came to get dinner. I shouldn't let my food get cold. Have a good night."

She turned on her heel and walked out of the bar as if she hadn't just shown up out of nowhere after three months. He hadn't even known she was back in town, let alone expected to see her in Dare's bar. They hadn't made any promises to each other. There had been no last names, no judgments, no backstories. But he knew almost every single person in his town who wasn't a tourist, and Melody hadn't been one of them. And yet, she was back and ordering food as if she had been here all along. Once again, he ignored his brother's look and packed up his things. He wasn't going to follow her, but he would go home and have some time to himself. He wasn't in the mood for questions, didn't feel like dealing with knowing looks and smiles. Because the best night of his life had just walked out the door. Again. And he still only knew her first name.

And from what he'd just seen, their night together hadn't left the same impression on her.

Who knew an evening without whiskey could be so revealing.

Chapter 3

Melody Waters rested her head on her closed door and forced herself to take a deep breath. She hadn't meant to start off her new life quite as drastically as it had happened but, apparently, the blood in her veins would allow nothing less. She couldn't just be normal and stay under the radar. She was officially her parents' daughter and her grandmother's granddaughter. If she really thought about it, she'd been that long before coming to Whiskey.

She had only been in town for a week, or rather *back* in town, and she was already running away from situations that were far too awkward for her to deal with. Honestly, she couldn't believe she'd actually lasted a whole week without seeing Fox. She thought she'd done a good job of hiding her reaction to seeing him again, but for all she knew, he had seen right through the mask she'd forced onto her face. Well, he had seen every other part of her, why not see through her façade?

But Fox wasn't the reason she'd moved. He was just a bad

mistake for one night that happened to be the most delicious mistake in a long line of mistakes. And if she thought the word *mistake* one more time tonight, she'd end up going for another glass of whiskey herself.

She held back a shiver at the thought of sipping whiskey, since the last time she had done that, she'd licked it off Fox's lips. The liquor had been smooth and smoky and tasted even better off him. Not that she would ever tell him that or even think about it again. Because she was moving on from that phase of her life. There would no longer be another one-night stand for her to try and forget or any more strings of relationships she ran away from because she was so afraid of the person she once was.

Melody had moved to this small town in Pennsylvania because her grandma needed her, but also because Melanie needed her grandma. Her grandmother might be able to do a lot on her own, but she wasn't getting any younger—or so she kept saying—so Melody was here to help out. And because of that, it would also be Melody's fresh start. It had taken her far too long to figure out what this new life of hers could be, but now she was sitting in a building she *owned*.

She wasn't a renter and didn't have to answer to anyone except the bank. With her contractors' help, and her own sweat and most likely tears, she was going to turn this empty set of rooms into a dance studio. She was not only certified, but she was in a far better place emotionally than she had been when she was first cast out into the cruel, harsh world.

If anyone had told her even a year ago that she would be opening up a dance studio in small-town Pennsylvania, she'd have called them crazy. But here she was, doing the one thing she'd never thought to do, and the one thing her grandma thought would be best for her. Melody was still undecided.

Whiskey seemed to have a little bit of everything within its town borders, and the tourists helped make it what it was. She didn't know the entire history of it, but she knew her grandma would probably explain it to her. Apparently, the town had been in the bootleg business with whiskey back in the days of Prohibition—or so they said. She didn't know if that was the actual truth, but the stories sounded just right for the tourists who came and wanted to get a little bit of history with a touch of flair. Plus, the town was adorable and made you feel as if you were at home even if you were only passing through.

Melody never truly had a home before this. And though her grandma had always invited her to visit, she had done her best to stay away. In retrospect, she didn't really know why she had done that other than the fact that she hadn't been a very good person. She made horrible decisions and mistakes, and through one careless act after another, she had been forced to pay for them.

But so had others.

Melody swallowed that hurt and pushed those thoughts from her mind. There was no room for that line of logic or those memories in her new life and this new place. She had picked up her dinner, caught an old friend who wasn't really a friend but more of a sweet temptation, and was now going to eat alone in her empty room while she imagined exactly what it could be. The building wasn't entirely empty since she'd had her contractors working on it for over a month now. But in the next couple of weeks, it would be her job to add the little touches that were just Melody. Soon, she'd be able to have a grand opening.

And…she was so freaking nervous, she knew she might throw up if she didn't take a breath.

She hadn't spent the past three weeks in Whiskey sitting on her hands. She had been finalizing her move so she could move in with her grandma and help around the house, and had done a lot of the legwork for opening up the studio. It wasn't as if she could just hang up a sign and people would suddenly flock in for classes and send their children in for instruction. She'd had to set up a social media presence and print flyers and even go into the community center to make sure everyone knew that she was opening up the studio for locals and tourists alike.

And even though she had countless business classes and years of study under her belt, she still felt as if she were barely treading water, ready to drown at any moment.

And it didn't help that she was an outsider moving in to this small town with its close community, opening up a business they didn't have before. She was also the long-lost granddaughter of the crazy lady of Whiskey, Pennsylvania.

Okay, that wasn't fair. Grandma Pearl wasn't crazy, but she had an aura of mystery and a sense of grandiosity around her. Apparently, a lot of people in town didn't really know much about her—unless Ms. Pearl wanted them to know.

Her grandmother had never been that person to Melody, though. She'd always been Grandma Pearl with the yummy candies, pretty feathers, and funny stories that used to make her laugh and dream of dancing.

Melody put her hand on her stomach and tried to calm her breathing. For someone who was about to teach others the art of dance and the seriousness and stoicism that came with that, she wasn't doing a very good job of it with herself.

"Okay, you can do this. Just eat dinner and soak in the atmosphere so you're ready to become the best instructor

Whiskey has ever seen. It doesn't matter that you're the only instructor in dance that Whiskey has seen in over a decade. And…now I'm sitting here alone in a barely lit room full of mirrors talking to myself. We just need a clown to finish the nightmare, and me standing in front of my class naked. Because, of course, that's what would happen. I wouldn't be wearing a tutu and ballet slippers. Instead, I'd be screaming and running in fear. And now, I just need to shut up."

She dipped into a plié, only slightly hindered by her skinny jeans, before sinking down to the floor completely with her food. After her mental ramble, she had thoughts of chainsaw-wielding clowns in her mind, so she forced herself not to look into the mirror. She would spend her first full evening in her new town in a place she owned, eating food that was totally bad for her. Since she had spent twenty years of her life not being able to eat what she wanted, she planned to enjoy her onion rings in peace. Clowns in mirrors or not.

And since her grandma was out with her bridge club, Melody knew she wouldn't be missing anything at home. It was still awkward that as an adult she was moving into her elderly grandmother's house, but that was what her grandma had wanted, and frankly, Melody needed the interaction. Eventually, she would find her own place when she knew her grandma was steady enough. Melody had a feeling that Pearl didn't need her at all, and had, in fact, only invited her to stay for Melody's benefit, but she wasn't going to fight it. Not anymore. She had fought long enough. Now, she was home. Wherever this new home of hers was.

Now that she was sitting and enjoying her very greasy yet amazing onion rings, she couldn't get a particular face out of her mind. And it had nothing to do with her grandma or dancing.

When she came to visit her grandma and the place Pearl had picked out for her, she had been a little overwhelmed by all the decisions ahead of her. Her grandma had sent her out to have a little fun—but not *too much.* Melody had done enough of that before everything changed. Of course, she hadn't realized how quickly whiskey could hit her system when she wasn't used to it, or how Fox could do the same to her.

He had smiled at her, and she had been lost. It wasn't as if an attractive man hadn't ever smiled at her before. Fox was far from the first, but there was something in his eyes that had sent warmth straight through her. He had taken shot for shot with her, and soon, they were talking close, leaning closer, drinking a little too much, and finally stumbling their way to his place. Thankfully, Whiskey wasn't all that big, and Fox had lived near enough to walk.

They'd had the hottest night of her life, ripping buttons from shirts, biting and licking and scoring nails on skin. She held back a moan just thinking about it, even though she knew she had to push him and his taste from her mind. She hadn't meant to sleep with anybody when she came to visit but, apparently, her body—and her mind if she were honest with herself—hadn't been able to hold back with Fox. Before he told her that his brother owned the bar, she'd sort of hoped that he was just a tourist and she would never have to see him again when she moved to town. But all of that was thrown out the window when he mentioned who owned the bar. He had even pointed out his entire family and group of friends to her, even though she was a little too far gone to remember everybody's face or name.

He hadn't taken advantage of her, though. He'd been just as far gone, and if anything, they had taken advantage of each other. And they had been safe, using a condom each time to make sure there wouldn't be any surprises. It had helped that she was also on birth control—not that she'd told him that since she hadn't wanted to fight him on the whole condom issue. She didn't actually know if Fox would have, but other guys had in the past, and she knew how to protect herself. Either way, they'd loved on each other, lusted after each other, and had fallen asleep sweaty and in each other's arms. And when she woke the next morning, she had quietly stolen one of his shirts, stuffed herself into her jeans, and tiptoed out of his house after leaving a note. She had done her best to clean herself up, but she knew that others knew a walk of shame when they saw one. She just hoped no one recognized her now.

She'd needed a fresh start, and she was afraid she might have screwed that up with a single intense night with one of the sweetest men she had ever met.

She had done a decent job of the brush-off, she thought, but if she were going to stay in this new town, she needed to grow a pair and talk to Fox like a human being.

She just hoped it wouldn't be as awkward as it already felt.

Chapter 4

The next morning, Melody stood in her grandma's kitchen, coffee in hand, and tried to pry her eyes fully open. When she had dance practice and strength workouts before dawn back in the day, she'd been able to wake up easily. Or at least far easier than she was now since it took over an hour of coffee, a shower, and far too many yawns for her liking to actually feel like a human being.

She'd stayed late at her studio the night before after she finished her dinner. Clown nightmares aside, she'd gotten a lot of work done on the places the contractors had finished so she could make it her own. She'd ended up getting so far into it that she'd stayed later than she planned. By the time she'd gotten home, her grandma had already returned and had gone to bed. She'd left Melody a note, but Melody still felt like a jerk for not being there for her grandma. That was one of the main reasons she'd chosen Whiskey as her home, and she felt as if she were already failing at it.

Melody had spent the first years of her life never failing,

always working hard to succeed. Nowadays, she never seemed to be able to work hard enough *not* to fail.

"I need more coffee for this," she mumbled. She was thinking far too deeply on only one cup of caffeine. Her grandma would be down any minute to get breakfast for herself, so Melody went into the fridge and at least prepared what she could for her. Grandma Pearl liked her cup of yogurt and a half of grapefruit every morning, without fail. Sometimes, she'd add a spoonful of granola to the yogurt for kicks, but other than that, her grandma had been having this same breakfast since the eighties.

Melody held back a shudder. She'd had something similar for her first meal of the day years ago when her parents and coach had allowed to her have dairy. And then they'd moved her to the latest fad diet to keep her weight off while she danced. There was no way she'd be able to stomach yogurt this early in the morning, and perhaps any time of the day since the idea of that texture in her mouth made her want to hurl.

On that pleasant note, she finished setting up her grandma's breakfast and headed into the living room with her second cup of coffee so she could work on her laptop. She had a few social media things to do every day to make sure her presence was out there, and while she scheduled some of her posts, she couldn't do them all like that. Plus, she was waiting on a few emails from those who ran the community center, as well as the mayor's office since the town's executive branch had a hand in everything its residents did. Melody didn't mind since the people she'd talked to had been really helpful in helping her set up her place. She just hoped they continued to like her once the doors were open and classes began. She perused a few emails, swallowed hard when she read one from the mayor that was actually good news—if a bit stressful—and ignored the rest. At least for now.

She chugged another gulp of her coffee since it was cool enough and opened her website from the back end. Today was the day she opened the official sign-ups for her dance classes. She planned to do a multitude of levels that either met weekly or daily in some cases, and she needed *people* to fill it. She'd been waiting on the okay from the mayor's office to open it up, and now that she had that email in her inbox, she could officially open for business—at least online.

And…maybe she wouldn't throw up.

Maybe.

She quickly hit the commands on her site so she could open the forms. She didn't have an extensive knowledge of website design, but at least for the start, she could do the small bits. If and when her business actually took off, she would be able to hire someone to make it look a little more professional. But for now, her sleepless nights and extra website building classes had paid off, and she was able to at least put out some form of product. She honestly didn't know how she had come from wanting to dance professionally with dreams of becoming a prima ballerina to opening her own studio and dealing with all the business and math that came with that. She swallowed hard once again, remembering that it had, in fact, been her fault she was down this path to begin with. And now she just had to deal with the consequences. Just like she'd been doing for the past few years. Or, at least now, doing better than she had been.

She hit save on the page and went to look at it live on her site. It was all there, the form open and ready for sign-ups. She would also have paper sign-ups at the community center, and at her studio where she planned to leave the door open while she worked on setting up. Hopefully, word of mouth would spread, and she would have more than just herself staring at a mirror with a ballet barre. Oh, God, she really, really hoped that.

She went back to her emails and sent the website link once again to the community center and to the mayor's office, just in case. They already had the link, but now that she could say it was live with the form open, maybe they'd be able to help.

Just as she was about to close the browser, an incoming email made her pause. She frowned at the subject line that said *You* and nothing else. It was from an unfamiliar address, but instead of deleting it like she probably should have, she opened it instead. And froze.

I know what you did.

She blinked once, twice, then closed her browser and shut off her computer. She could hear her heartbeat echoing in her eardrums as she fought to control her breathing. It was nothing. Just spam that she should have deleted before she even opened the damn email. But something in the back of her mind told her that it wasn't just a joke; wasn't just a wrong email.

There was a reason she had been running all this time.

And while she wasn't hiding any longer, she prayed that her past hadn't once again found her.

And now she was just being silly over a weird spam email that had nothing to do with her.

"Melody, darling, thank you so much for my breakfast. Would you like me to make you something?"

Melody turned at the sound of her grandma's voice and smiled. Her grandma was larger than life packaged in a barely five-foot, stunning woman. She didn't appear her age

—a number Melody wasn't sure of. She knew her grandmother had given birth to her mother later in life, and she had to be old enough to at least know the Rat Pack—at least according to local and family legend—but other than that, she honestly did not know how old the other woman was. Not that it mattered in the end, because no matter what, her grandmother was the only family she had left, and that meant she would cherish whatever time they had together. Because even though Grandma Pearl looked as though she could take on armies with her curves and grin, there was a reason Melody had come to Whiskey, and it wasn't just for her own problems and business.

"I'm okay with coffee for now, Grandma. Thank you." Melody set her mug and her computer down on the coffee table and stood up so she could wrap her arms around her grandmother. They were about the same height, but Pearl seemed so much frailer than she had just three months ago. Maybe, though, that was all just in Melody's head because she was worried and needed to feel needed—selfish as it was.

"You need something more than coffee," Pearl said with a raised brow. A brow that had already been perfectly drawn in with precision, Melody knew that it had taken years of practice to get it just right.

"Oh, I know, and I'm going to get a piece of fruit and maybe some oatmeal or something. Or maybe an egg white since I don't know if I can stomach oatmeal right now." Maybe it was just nerves, but her stomach had been out of sorts for the past month or so. She really hoped that once her studio was open and she had people coming in and out the doors, her nerves would finally settle down. But knowing the blood that ran in her veins, that probably wouldn't ever happen.

Pearl patted her cheek and smiled. "Okay, honey, as long as you are taking care of yourself as well as you are taking care of me. I am so happy that you're here. It's been a long time since I had someone else walking through these halls who wasn't just here to help me clean them. Because, Melody, no matter how many times I say I can handle cleaning this monstrosity of a house by myself, I know that, in the end, I need a little help with the elbow grease. Why spend all my days scrubbing toilets by myself when I can ask for little help and enjoy the sun on my face later. I deserve it, don't I?"

"Of course, you do." Her grandma had worked up until a few years ago. Yes, she had retired from her life as a showgirl many moons ago, but her grandma had always held down a job and still volunteered to help others. The family had money, and that was how Pearl had been able to afford this house to begin with, but Melody had learned from her grandmother that even if you had all the money in the world, you still had to learn what that money meant. Her parents, while loving in their own ways, hadn't taught her that. Instead, they'd put all of their energy into her dancing, and when that career choice hadn't panned out the way any of them wanted, things had never been the same. And then there wasn't time to fix that.

She quickly pushed those thoughts from her mind, knowing that this wasn't the time to go down that path. She had known when she opened her studio, or at least started the process of it, that those memories would come back in full force, but she wasn't ready to deal with them. And that meant repressing everything. Her psychiatrist would have a field day when she finally made another appointment, but for now, she would focus on her grandmother, her new business, and this new town.

She helped her grandma around the house for a little bit and made sure Pearl was set up with her book and a nice cup of tea outside so she could spend the rest of her morning in nature like she had wanted, and then Melody quickly got ready for her day. Since she would be working inside a very dusty studio as the rest of her contract team got everything set up for opening day, she didn't bother putting on anything too nice. Just old, form-fitting jeans, and a floral top that wasn't her favorite but would get the job done.

By the time she made it to her studio, her nerves had settled down, but she was really ready to get elbow-deep in work so she could focus on that instead of her memories and the email from earlier that wouldn't quite leave her mind.

Before she could open her door, though, a big man with even bigger muscles stood by her building, a broody expression on his face. She almost went for her keys so she could gouge out his eyes if he attacked her, but she stopped when she saw a familiar smirk on his lips for a bare instant.

She had seen that smile, but on another face, and she realized she had indeed seen this man before, too. Fox had pointed him out at the bar that fateful night. This was his brother, Loch. She couldn't quite remember if he was older or younger than Fox, but now that she got closer to him, she saw the similarities in their features. Fox had darker hair and was slightly more slender in build. Plus, Fox never really had that brooding expression on his face, at least not from what she had seen in their too-short time together.

"Hello? Can I help you?" She pretended as if she didn't actually know who he was because she wasn't honestly sure how she and Fox would play this whole thing between them. She wasn't very good at subterfuge, so she would probably make a mistake and end up telling his brother everything, but at least for an introduction, she might not work herself into circles.

"Melody, right? The new studio owner? I'm Loch. I own the security firm and the gym next door."

"Security and the gym? How do you sleep if you do both?" He just stared at her, and she blinked. "I mean, hi, Loch. Yes, I'm Melody. And you're standing in front of what eventually will be my dance studio."

He gave her a nod, studying her face as if he were memorizing every detail. Fox had done the same, but she knew for a fact that it had been done with very different intent. If Loch were in the so-called security business, he was probably making sure he could pick her out of a lineup. And at that demeaning thought, she let out a breath.

"Nice to meet you. The gym is my full-time job, I do some training in self-defense and other classes that I thought the town might need over time. And since we are such a small community, I'm the only one qualified right now to add in security systems and other things like that. So, if you want something for your studio, let me know. I know you have the Henderson boys working on your place for contracting. They're the best of the best, so you chose well there. But if you find yourself in need of a handyman and can't get into the Hendersons' schedule, give me a call. I'm right next door."

Melody's eyes widened. "You do all of that? You really are a Jack of all trades."

Lock smiled and, this time, it went all the way to his eyes. It made him look a lot hotter, though still not as sexy as Fox. And she needed to stop thinking like that.

"I started in security years ago before I moved back to town. I opened the gym because I needed a job. The handyman thing came because my brothers and sister and I constantly broke shit when we were kids. Someone needed to figure out how to fix it all so my mother wouldn't wring our necks. I actually didn't come over here to sell you my business like I just did, though. I just can't help myself, apparently."

"So why did you come over?" It seemed to her that Loch had a lot of layers, and if she were in a place to deal with that—and hadn't already slept with his brother and was trying to ignore that connection—she might've wanted to figure out how to peel those layers back. But as it was, he was so not for her.

"Mostly to welcome you to Whiskey. And to say that I don't know how you're planning to get clients to your studio—though I figure since you're opening the business you probably already have a detailed plan—but if you want more business, I have people constantly coming in and out of my gym. I figured we're both in the same sphere, so we might as well figure out how to work together. I don't offer dance as a form of exercise or even an art at the gym since I'm not qualified and have two left feet, but if you want, we can work together to try and help out the citizens of Whiskey and each other."

She hadn't been expecting that and couldn't help the warm feeling that spread through her at the thought of such a welcome. Not a single person had stood in her way so far, and now they were literally opening their arms and trying to help her. She swallowed back a knot of emotion in her throat and tried to smile as if a hundred different things weren't going through her head at that very moment.

"Thank you so much. I just opened my sign-up forms today, actually. I haven't checked if anyone has signed up because I've been a little too nervous to look and possibly see it completely empty. But I put up flyers with the mayor and with the community center, too. If you let me, I'll give you a stack as well for the gym. I don't know how I could possibly repay you, but I'll figure out a way."

"We'll make it work. The place that will now be your studio has been reincarnated into a few different things over the years. For once, I would really like it to actually stay and be something the town needs."

They talked for a few more minutes, and then she finally walked into her studio after saying goodbye, her nerves even more on edge than usual. It seemed that people were talking about her new dance studio, and she had no idea what that meant. If Loch wanted her to succeed, could that mean that others wanted her to, as well? Or were they just waiting to watch her fail like she had failed at so many other things?

On that thought, her nerves finally got the best of her, and she ran to her newly finished bathroom, ignoring the looks of the guys working on one of the sections of her studio, and threw up in her pristine toilet.

Well, at least she had christened it herself thanks to her nerves and whatever had been going on with her stomach for the past month or so. She had moved to town, trying to change her life, and if her body let her, she might just make it work. At least, she hoped.

Chapter 5

Fox loved his job, loved the days when he could focus on his projects and not just other writers' copy, and he had a feeling today was going to be one of the days he remembered. Always. At least, that's what he hoped. He'd been working on his research for Ms. Pearl and the piece he wanted to do on her for a few days now, though he'd had the idea for the story for a couple of years. He'd been waiting until the time was right, and Ms. Pearl was ready to share. He'd finished the other two editorials that would go out in the next two weeks since he didn't write full articles like he was doing now every day. In fact, this would be one of his longest pieces if he had anything to say about it. His goal was to make it like a series for two or even four weeks over the next few months. From what he could tell from what he'd dug up on this woman with such a rich backstory, if she let him, she could be a whole book on her own. Fox didn't write novels, though, so perhaps he would just make her story a serial that people could come back to.

All of this, of course, was just in his head until he heard the stories directly from her lips. Until then, he wouldn't know exactly what he had beyond a short biography.

His nerves didn't help matters, and he hadn't been sleeping well at all since he saw Melody at the bar a few evenings ago. He'd been shocked as hell that she was not only back in town, but, according to Loch, also moving here permanently. Apparently, she was opening up a dance studio next to his brother's gym. He didn't know when that decision had happened, but apparently, he should've asked more questions. However, at the time, he'd been memorizing every single curve on Melody's body.

Jesus, he really needed to get his head out of the gutter and on to his work. Just because she was moving back to town didn't mean she wanted anything to do with him. And, frankly, he wasn't sure what he wanted if the option presented itself to him. Their evening together was only supposed to be a single whiskey-filled night. Yet he couldn't get her out of his mind. And, now, she was in his town, and perhaps in his life permanently. She would be working right next door to his brother. The damn building next door to where he went four times a week to work out. He wasn't a gym rat, and frankly wasn't as strong as either of his brothers, but he hated to be left behind. And his sister trained even more than he did thanks to her husband. He was slowly falling behind on the athletic curve, but that was nothing new when it came to him. He'd always been the one in his books and his words while trying to catch up with his gangly arms and legs that he felt were just now getting toned.

And now he was once again letting his thoughts wander to every single thing except for what was important: his work. He was on his way to Ms. Pearl's home where, hopefully, she would regale him with stories of her past and the rich life he knew she had led. Still led if he were honest. He didn't want the story to just be a bullet point list of the people she had met or the places she danced before she came to their small Pennsylvania town. He wanted to hear the inflections in her voice and see the light in her eyes as she spoke about it so everyone could hear and see who she was when she had lived that life.

He wanted to crack open the truth and find out more about this very interesting woman. And though it was his job as a reporter to sometimes dig beneath that first layer and find the ugly truths, he didn't want this story to be about that either. He wasn't in the habit of hurting those he wrote about, making them face something they would rather not confront again.

Finding the delicate balance was a talent he had honed over time, and something he thought perhaps he could excel at one day. So he would tell this woman's story and show the world that there was more to their neighbor than met the eye. And while doing that, he would make sure she knew that he valued her time and her life, and would do his best to honor the trust she was putting in him. Others had tried to interview her before, and she had said no. But for some reason, she had come to *him* with her story, even though he had been thinking about it before that. He was going to do his best to show her how grateful he was.

That was how he found himself sitting in his car in her driveway, taking notes as he looked at her sprawling house that was set off one of the connecting streets off Main Street. Whiskey had one main thoroughfare where most of the shops and restaurants were located. It made it easy for tourists to walk from place to place, shopping and grabbing food and drinks as they filled the town's coffers. The town survived on tourism, and he'd never take that for granted. His brother's bar was right off Main Street, while Loch's and Melody's businesses, as well as his own, were off side roads that could all easily be seen from multiple directions off Main. The founding fathers of Whiskey had set each street at a diagonal, so it was easy to see the buildings that were in the direct line of Main Street. But that meant giving directions that had anything to do with north or south or even east or west was a little trickier than it should've been.

Fox lived in a small house a couple of streets off Main Street. That meant he could walk to most of the establishments, as well as his job. He could've walked today, too, but he'd chosen to drive because rain was in the forecast, and he really didn't want to get any of his notes or his computer wet.

Ms. Pearl's home was one of the original houses from back before Prohibition. The architecture in itself was art that took his breath away. Loch would probably know more about the exact era and everything that had to do with every single brick and turret, but Fox could still appreciate the beauty and history that came with the building. Ms. Pearl's family wasn't the original owner since she had bought the place from the great-great-great-grandchild of the original owner or something like that. But, now, she was her own history within the very historical town, and that was just one more thing he was going to try to portray to the best of his abilities in his piece.

He didn't take any photos since he knew he wanted to speak to her first and make sure they had laid out the ground rules before he started his article. But he had a feeling that past and present photos of the extraordinary woman wouldn't be the only highlights of what he was about to write. Because her home was as eccentric and graceful as she was.

He walked up to the door and rang the doorbell that made a loud gong sound, and he couldn't help but smile. Of course, a house like this would have a very unique doorbell.

Ms. Pearl opened the door herself, surprising him. For all her mystery and aura, he had figured she would have staff to do that for her. Instead, the woman herself, the subject of his piece, stood in front of him, all five feet of her looking as if she could take on the world even at her undisclosed age. One thing Fox did not plan to do was ask her age. Not only had he learned never to do that, his mother would also beat the hell out of him for even thinking about it. And he wanted to make sure that Pearl kept some air of mystery even if she told him a lot of her secrets so he could tell the world. He liked the idea that no one knew her exact age, and that she could've lived in any century, any era, and been the star of any of them. It could've just been his writer's mind at work, but he didn't care. He was going to thread that into the story and make sure the world knew that you could make a difference at any age.

"Mr. Collins, I'm so glad you're here. And on time. I really do love that in a man. And, boy, do I have stories to tell you about men who knew what to do with their time." She winked, and he couldn't help the deep belly laugh that came at her words. She joined him in laughter and took a step back, gesturing for him to enter the house.

"Call me Fox." He did his best to call her Ms. Pearl in his head, even though sometimes he couldn't help but call her Pearl. He didn't even know her surname because she had spent so long going by "Ms. Pearl" to the world, that everyone had just assumed it *was* her last name. But he knew that Pearl was her first name and that she kept her last name under wraps for only her family and her lawyer. Not that he knew too much about her family. That was one thing she had kept secret, and it was something he wasn't sure if he wanted to unravel for her. There were some confidences that should be kept, and even as a reporter, he'd learned that lesson long ago.

"Well, Fox. Welcome to my home." At her words, he couldn't help but look around and be entranced by the building he walked into. Someone, perhaps the woman herself, had taken great pains to restore every inch of the house. Large, arched, wooden columns stood by the doorway, creating an even grander entrance for those who walked beneath them. There were heavy drapes on the tall windows that practically took up the entire back wall across from where he stood. But the curtains didn't look too ornate or fussy for the house. They had been drawn back so light filled the room and made the house look even larger—yet homier at the same time. He wasn't sure if he would ever be able to describe the beauty and warmth of the house he now stood in. And while there were modern conveniences that he could spot throughout the home, there were still historical edges on every piece he could see. His mother would probably weep at the beauty of it and want to sit down and hear about every single inch of history and architecture. Her favorite shows were always the house-building and selling shows where they went back and restored some of the older homes rather than just carrying out what might not work now for modern convenience. He had a feeling the woman at his side and his mother would probably agree on a lot. And because he knew that his mom was a force to be reckoned with, he was a little afraid to ever introduce them beyond how they might know each other already. It was a small town, after all.

"Your home is beautiful."

She beamed at him and looked even younger than she already did. Seriously, he had no idea how she could look so radiant for someone who had to be in her late seventies, if not older. Either a plastic surgeon with the skills of a god had gotten to her face, or she had won the lottery with care and genetics.

He could still see laugh lines around her eyes and mouth, however. And for that, he knew he'd fallen just a bit more in love with Ms. Pearl—not that he'd ever tell her that.

"Thank you," she said, her smile reaching her eyes even more. "I find it beautiful, as well. Would you like a tour before we get started? I'm sure I can tell you a few things about the place, though my lawyer has every single inch detailed down to the bones if you would like that information. I find that a little too dry for my taste. I'm sure as I give you the tour, however, we can talk about the logistics of exactly what the two of us will be doing for the time being." She took his outstretched arm and patted his bicep.

She didn't make her words sound sexual at all, but he could hear an almost seductive quality to her tone. *It isn't sexual,* he thought again, It was more that the woman was all warmth and smoothness like whiskey, wrapped around someone who knew exactly who she was, what she wanted, and how to get it. And he admired the hell out of her for it.

"I think that can be arranged. I would love a tour. You know, the town has legends written and spread about this house and the woman who inhabits it. The fact that you keep the mystery well and true has only aided that myth."

She tossed her head back and laughed. "You know, I do

spend my mornings with my cup of tea figuring out exactly how to weave my web of mystery and lies so the town has something to talk about. I'm a regular femme fatale."

"So I hear." He said it so deadpan that Ms. Pearl stopped right in her tracks and gave him a look.

"You know, I'm interested in hearing what kinds of stories you've already heard about me, Fox. I'm sure I have even juicier tales for you. Alas, I am merely an old woman locked in a dusty mansion, wandering about in my nightgown, scaring the small children of this quaint Pennsylvania town."

Fox couldn't help the snort that escaped. "Unless you play that role on Halloween, I'm pretty sure nobody except the weirdest members of our town would actually believe that if I wrote it."

She shrugged as if she hadn't a care in the world. "Quite true. And I only played the woman in the attic once. Perhaps I will again this year just to see who screams at my mere presence. Now, let me see, what stories have you heard? Is it the time I danced for the king? What king? That will have to wait until we get to know each other a little bit more. Or was it the time I ran naked down the strip, the mob on my tail—so to speak—as I held two bags of money with large dollar signs printed on the front? At the time, I did not have the Clyde to my Bonnie, unless you're hearing the wrong stories."

Fox shook his head, knowing she was playing with him, trying to figure out exactly how this interview would go. He didn't mind that, and was well prepared. It wasn't as if he hadn't had tough interviews before.

"I'm guessing only part of that is true, even though I have heard both of those stories. When our town isn't drinking whiskey and discussing the days of Prohibition and everything that came with that, they're pretty much discussing exactly what happens with you. Or rather, what *happened* with you."

"That, and what happens to the Collins family. I hear congratulations are in order, not only for your little sister but for Dare, as well. I heard that right, didn't I? Little Tabby is all married and having a baby with someone out in Denver? And our Dare has fallen for his innkeeper." She gave him a somber look as she turned to face him. "I will say, as much as I joke about being the center of attention in this town, I truly wish the town hadn't been forced to focus on what happened to them and the bar. Dare and Kenzie are okay though, right? I know Kenzie's ex-husband is behind bars, but he deserves so much more than that for hurting that little girl."

That she'd called Kenzie a little girl just reiterated the fact that Ms. Pearl was ageless.

Fox took her hand and gave it a slight squeeze. It seemed so fragile beneath his palm that he didn't want to add any more pressure than he already had. "Kenzie and Dare are fine. They're in love and talking about marriage and possibly more babies to add to the horde. The bar is fine after that slight incident, as well, and the asshole—pardon my French—who dared to think he could hurt my family is no longer a problem."

He clenched his jaw and forced himself to relax for fear he'd end up scaring the poor woman with how angry he got just thinking about those who'd come for his family.

"I'm glad to hear it. Everybody deserves their happily ever after, even if it might not be quite what they thought it would be at first. Now, let me show you the house so we can talk about what kinds of stories will be told. And though I like to hear the embellishments that people speak of me, I do think, perhaps it's time to air a bit of truth rather than just the mystery surrounding the myth."

He relaxed at her words and followed her around as she told him a little bit about the history of the building and talked about exactly what they were going to work on. It would take time, he figured. This wouldn't be a one-and-done interview, not when it came to this woman and her life. She deserved far more than a simple byline about a woman who had a story to tell. Her words about truth rather than mystery couldn't have made him happier. Because as much as he loved the larger-than-life idea of her, he really wanted to get to know the woman behind the coy smiles and the showgirl feathers.

They were just about finished when Ms. Pearl gestured towards the living room once again, the sound of someone walking through the other side of the house hitting Fox's ears. "I see my granddaughter is home. I'd love for you to meet her. She's just moved to town to stay with me, and I'm thrilled. She's a piece of my heart, you know. I'm honored that she's taking time out of her life to spend it with an old woman."

A very familiar voice filled the air, and he did his best not to react. "Yes, because it's such a chore spending time with my favorite person in the world. And I cannot believe you just called yourself an old woman."

Ms. Pearl winked and held out her arm. "Fox, I'd love for you to meet my granddaughter, Melody. Melody, this is Fox, that reporter I told you about."

Fox had no idea how Melody wanted to play this. Did she want her grandmother to know that the two of them had already met? No one else needed to know how intimately they knew each other, but keeping secrets from the start never ended well. He would let her decide what steps they took since this was her family and not his.

"Hi, Fox, nice to see you again." She smiled, but for some reason, it didn't reach her eyes. From the pallor of her face, however, he had a feeling it had nothing to do with him and everything to do with how she was feeling. Was she sick? He would have to ask once he got time alone with her. He didn't want to alert her grandmother and possibly worry her for no reason.

"You two know each other? Really?" The older woman drew out the last word, and Fox had a feeling he was going to be in trouble if he weren't careful.

"Yes, Grandmother, we met at his brother's bar when I first came to town to visit, and again at the same bar when I went to pick up my food. Dare's onion rings are to die for."

"True," Fox said, relieved that she was sticking to the truth if not the whole truth. He hated lying.

"Though he didn't ever mention to me that he was planning to report on you."

Fox held up his hands. "I didn't know the two of you were related or I probably would've mentioned it."

"Oh, I know you would have. I was more worried about the fact that my grandmother never actually explained to me what kind of report you're doing on her. I will not have her hurt, Fox."

"Melody," Ms. Pearl chided.

Fox shook his head. "No, it's okay. I understand where she's coming from. I'm not here to bamboozle your grandmother, try to steal her money, or tell lies about her. Ms. Pearl approached me about telling some of her life story. I say *some*, even though she didn't because I have a feeling she wants to keep some secrets to herself. I'm fine with that because, unlike some reporters, I know there's a line. I'm not going to hurt your grandmother, Melody. I can promise you that. She has lived a rich life and wants to share just a little bit of it. She's an important icon to this town, and I'm honored that I get to show exactly what she means to this community—and possibly what this town means to her."

Melody's eyes filled with an emotion he couldn't read, but it was Ms. Pearl who dabbed at her eyes with a handkerchief.

"I knew I chose the right person for the job." She patted his shoulder and moved to kiss her granddaughter's cheek. "Now, I must go take my nap because, sadly, I'm at that age where I need naps during the day. I take solace in the fact that children do the same when they're of an age, as well. I look forward to seeing you at our next meeting, Fox. I'll have my people call yours to set it up." Then she walked away, leaving Melody and him alone in the living room.

He stuffed his hands into his pockets, unsure what to do with himself. "I didn't know you'd be here. Truly."

Melody gave him a shrug, her face just as pale as he'd seen it when he first walked in. "I believe you. I'm just now realizing how small this town actually is."

He studied her face and frowned. "Are you okay? You look pale."

She rolled her eyes, her back stiffening. "Just what every girl wants to hear. I'm fine, Fox. I'm sure my grandmother will have her people…since she actually *has* people, which I find fascinating, call you. Now you know where I live, and I guess since Loch knows where I work, you do, too. No need to hide from each other. I want to make Whiskey my home, and I don't want to screw it up. Okay?"

He nodded in understanding. She didn't want to screw it up by screwing with him. He understood that. Honestly.

Because they were only supposed to be together for one night. And now it seemed as if they would have to fight whatever attraction the two of them clearly had for each other to keep it just that one night. She didn't want complications, and frankly, neither did he.

"I get you. Have a nice day, Melody."

"You too, Fox. Just, um, take care of my grandmother, okay?"

He met her gaze and nodded. "I will. I always take care of the people I care about. And I care about this town. Meaning, I care about you, too, Melody. I'm not going to make it complicated and messy by saying anything more than that, other than the fact that if you need me, I'm here. I'd like us to be friends because it seems as if we can't stop meeting each other like this."

She swallowed hard, and he watched the long line of her throat work. "Friends. I can do that. I think I could use a friend."

He didn't touch her, though something deep inside him wanted to. Instead, he said his goodbyes and walked out of the beautiful home with the two beautiful people living within it. This story had just gotten a little deeper, a bit more complicated. But this was his job, and he would figure out a way to make it work. And he hadn't been lying to Melody. He took care of those in his circle, and these two women were now in his circle. What that meant, he didn't know, but he was curious enough to find out.

Chapter 6

Melody couldn't believe how fast time seemed to be going. Okay, it had only been a day since she'd last seen Fox at her house, and two days since she had met Loch outside of her studio, but she still felt as if the days were passing far too quickly. Soon, her studio would open, and she would be teaching full-time at a place that she not only owned but had literally put her blood, sweat, and tears into. Okay, it had been a paper cut inside her building that counted as the blood, but it counted nonetheless. And if she took into account every single blood blister and cut from dancing hours and hours a day to hopefully one day become a prima ballerina, then that was a lot of blood, sweat, and tears indeed.

Her dreams of dancing for the New York City Ballet and not only becoming a soloist but also a principal dancer might be long gone, but she still hoped she could have dancing in her life. She wasn't the same person she was before everything had changed, but she still had the craft in her veins. Her grandmother had been a famous showgirl, using her hips, feathers, and legs to tell a story, even if others hadn't known exactly what she was saying. Her mother had been a dancer, as well, but had given up everything early when she thought she wasn't good enough. Melody didn't know if that was true, and her grandmother wouldn't tell her. But she had a feeling the drive her mother had with regards to Melody's career and talent had come from the fact that she had never lived out her own dreams.

Melody had spent her younger years in dance classes, strength classes, and more, not having a childhood outside of the path she had been set on in that early stage of her life. And though others had chosen the path for her, she had gone willingly when she found the passion in dance.

She had danced for some of the best teachers that were out there because of her talent and who her grandmother was, and she would never take those lessons and honors for granted. When she was accepted to Juilliard, she had thought her dreams were finally coming true, even at the tender age of eighteen. Then, everything had shattered around her, and she had been forced to figure out who she was without dance being her sole reason for living.

At one point, she'd never thought she would dance again, and had thrown away all of her old training leotards and pointe shoes in anger and misguided guilt. No, she couldn't quite seem misguided, could she? But that was another train of thought that she didn't want to think about today. Not when she had so much on her plate.

Speaking of work, she opened up her laptop and bit her lip. She had been a coward for not checking her sign-up form the past two days since she'd opened it. She also hadn't checked her emails beyond the important ones from the community center. The messages having to do with the dance studio that were attached to the form went to a separate email account she hadn't opened in two days. That strange note that had to be spam had been moved into a special folder just in case, but she figured it was nothing important. She wasn't special enough for an email like that anyway. Not anymore.

"If you want to be a businesswoman and be successful, you have to get your head out of your ass and check your freaking email. Don't be a coward, Melody Waters."

Now that she was talking to herself again in an empty home since her grandmother was out with Fox for a lunchtime interview, she knew she was close to jumping off the deep end. The fact that she also couldn't stop thinking about Fox and how…nice it had been to see him was neither here nor there.

If she realized that nobody was signing up for classes, she would have to try and figure out what she was going to do with the mortgage payments on an empty building that no one would ever walk into again.

And, of course, if she kept rambling in her head about her own worries, she wouldn't think about the fact that she hadn't been able to see Fox this morning because her grandmother had left to walk towards the restaurant area of town on her own. Melody had been more than ready to walk her grandmother but, apparently, Ms. Pearl was clearly able to do things herself. Melody still worried, but Fox had texted her when her grandmother showed up.

She hadn't given Fox her number, had been very careful not to do so that night and in the time she had seen him since, but Grandmother must have given it to him. She didn't mind, though she probably should have, but when she put him in her contacts under his name and not something too sexy or mean, she figured they were well on their way to being the friends they had talked about rather than anything more heated like her subconscious and her lady parts might want.

She took a deep breath and opened the spreadsheet that her form fed into. Then she stopped what she was doing and blinked a few times.

It wasn't empty.

It wasn't even close to empty.

There were over twenty sign-ups in just two days. How the hell had that happened? Well, it wasn't as if she didn't know exactly how that had happened since she had put in tons of work and so had the other people around her, but she hadn't thought this was possible. Not only were those twenty-plus people signed up for her classes, but they were also signed up for a variety of her classes. There were a set of children who wanted the beginner's classes—boys and girls that would be in a mixed class. There were also a few intermediate students who wanted extra classes on top of the ones they were already taking out of town with another instructor. Though she would have to consider carefully and talk to their teachers to make sure they not only didn't overwork themselves, but that they were all on the same page. As a child, Melody always had more than one instructor at a time, and it had helped to strengthen her dancing abilities. But she wanted to make sure that anyone she worked with was on the right path.

And even more amazing, there were a couple of adults who wanted to take a chance on the adult, beginners' ballet class. It wouldn't be for pure style or anything along the lines of what her intermediate or even the children would be doing. But there were some who wanted a class where they could learn the basic steps for flexibility, and others who wanted the class as more of a workout type of event. She had put both up as offerings and had them in her schedule, and it looked as if she would have at least a few in each class. She had a couple of additional classes that at least had two people in each, and she was beyond thrilled. The way she had scheduled her class load meant she would have about two or three classes per day, but nothing too strenuous on her physically. She didn't have the flexibility or strength she once had, especially since the incident, so she knew she couldn't put as much pressure on her body as she'd once been able to. But this way, she would have people coming in, her body would still get the exercise it needed, and her soul would still be attached to dance. The latter was something she hadn't known she needed until it had been ripped away from her so suddenly.

And because some classes would be in the morning, some in the afternoon, and others in the evening, she would always have room to add additional classes if there was ever a need or the time, and she would have time to do all the administrative and business stuff that came with owning her own studio, as well. And her grandmother would be happy to hear that she'd also scheduled in time to just *be*. She hadn't figured out exactly who she was without that one dream constantly at the forefront of her mind, but she was working on it. And moving to the small town and opening up a place just for herself was one way to get started.

Her hands were shaking by the time she went through each person to see what they had filled out in the form. She also had a few emails from concerned parents and even some of the adult dancers themselves who wanted to either return to dance or start again from scratch. She was of the firm belief that one was never too old to find their love for dance, even if that love of dancing might never lead to a career in it.

She went through and contacted each person, asking questions of her own and learning as much as she could from them without speaking or talking to them. She would learn what she would need as a teacher once she saw them move, and learn any limitations or strengths they had. She had one email from a concerned mother who had a daughter whom she hadn't signed up yet, but she wanted to talk to Melody personally about things. Her daughter was autistic but so in love with dance that she wanted to learn how to be a pretty ballerina. Melody's eyes watered at the love and protection in the mother's words, and knew that even if she had to open up a separate class for the little girl and work twice as hard, she would make sure she got to dance. Melody had actually taken a class on how to teach children with special needs, but knew she was nowhere near where she needed to be in order to give the girl everything she needed. That meant Melody would have to do a lot more studying and talk to the mother and anyone else in the child's life to make sure that they found the right routine and met the little girl's needs. She knew some children were fine working with others in the same room for a dance class, while some needed individual attention. Melody would just have to work out a way to make that happen. She didn't have the money to hire on another instructor right now, but that was in the business plan for later. When the time came, she would figure out what to do.

Melody immediately emailed back and told the woman exactly what she'd just thought, making sure that she knew that Melody was excited and honored about the opportunity to teach her daughter. Once again, she brushed tears from her eyes after she had finished the email. She'd been lucky growing up, being able to do things on her own without the help of others. But she had watched instructors berate those who couldn't get it in one try, and she refused to be that person. Everyone deserved a chance to be everything they could be, and it had taken her losing everything to realize exactly how much that meant.

Off-kilter, she finished answering her new emails, put up some new social media posts to get the word out, and set aside her computer. She needed to get back into the studio to finish decorating, but her contractor had said they needed time to finish putting up the last bits of paint and other touches that she would just be in the way for. And with all this new energy thanks to the wonderful news and daunting tasks ahead of her, she figured she might as well stay in shape because there was a lot of dancing to come.

Thanks to meeting her new neighbor, she knew exactly where she could go to work out. Hopefully, they would let her sign up for a gym membership because there was no way she would be able to stay in dancing shape by just doing yoga at her house and running outside every once in a while. At her age and with everything her body had been through with dance and then later after she was hurt, she needed to do strengthening exercises that she couldn't do at home. She knew her grandma would probably set up a whole gym in one of the various rooms that they had in the house if she had any idea that Melody needed it, but there was no way she was going to lean on her grandmother for that.

Making a decision, she cleaned up what she had left out since she still felt like a guest in her grandma's home, and went upstairs to change into her workout gear. When she got to Loch's place, she couldn't help but grin at the sign. It literally said Loch's Security and Gym. The man really did just about everything. She was half expecting a little add-on sign that said something about being a handyman but, apparently, that was just word of mouth.

When she walked in, Loch was behind the counter, scowling at something on his computer. He looked up as she made her way to him and let out a grunt. Not the most welcoming thing in the world, but it could have been worse. He could've literally shoved her out the door or something.

"Am I here at a bad time? I was wondering if I could sign up for a gym membership. Is that okay?"

Loch studied her before reaching under the desk in front of him and grabbing a stack of papers. "Sorry, having computer issues, and I'm getting annoyed. Not your problem, though. And, yeah, you can sign up for a gym membership. I don't do yearly or locked-in fees. We go month-to-month because I know not everybody's going to want to keep up with a gym membership for the whole year. We're not one of those big chains."

"That sounds perfect to me. But I'll probably be in here all year since I need to keep up with my strength if I'm going to be teaching next door. And while I can get most of it from dancing, I'll be more well-rounded if I do a full workout."

"Just fill out the paperwork, and you can get started today if you want." His gaze traveled over her clothes, and he gave her another nod. It didn't feel sexual in the least. Whereas she knew if his brother had done that to her, she'd heat from the inside out under the scrutiny. "You look like you're already in your gear, so I assume you want to work out today?"

"If I can. The guys next door are busy doing things I'll just get in the way of, so it's either this or twiddle my thumbs as I'm doing paperwork and wanting to bang my head against the table."

"Don't get me started on paperwork." He grumbled again and left her to fill out what she needed to. When she was done, she handed it over, and he handed her a temporary card and took her photo, saying he would send over her real card in the next day or two.

He went back to working on whatever he was doing on the computer, and she wondered if it had to do with the gym or the secret security firm that she really had no idea about. Maybe she'd been reading too much recently because her mind kept going to secret agents and spies rather than what was probably just a guy and his team who put up security systems and cameras for houses. She really needed to get a life rather than letting her imagination wander.

She was so busy in her head, that she didn't notice the man in front of her and slammed right into his very sweaty, very hard body.

She gripped his arms, his thigh going right between her legs as she pressed into him and looked up.

"Fox." She practically breathed the word, her pulse racing. Of course, she would run into Fox at his brother's gym. Of course, she would be clinging to him like a heroine in one of her favorite romance novels, her fingers digging into his biceps. Of course, his thigh would be pressed firmly against her crotch enough so he could probably feel the heat of her as she pulsated just from touching him—the day after they'd both promised each other they would just remain friends. Because this was Melody, and this was her life. What else could happen in a town named Whiskey with a man she'd had far too much whiskey with?

"Melody." His voice came out more like a growl than an

actual word, and he cleared his throat. "Melody, shit, I didn't see you. Did I hurt you?"

She hadn't let go of his arms, but he hadn't moved away from her either. She was aware that there were other people in the gym, but she knew they weren't looking at them. They were focused on their workouts and not the two of them clinging to each other as if they couldn't get enough.

And because she thought that particular thought, she let go of him and backed away. Her inner thighs missed Fox's touch immediately, but she ignored her traitorous lady parts and their needs and desires.

Damn them anyway. They always got her into trouble.

"I'm fine, and I'm the one who ran into you anyway." She swallowed hard, doing her best not to think about how exactly he'd felt pressed up against her. He fit far too perfectly, and she hoped the fact that she couldn't stop thinking about it was because she was hyped up for the gym.

And in terms of rationalizations, she'd just reached a new level.

He frowned. "If you're sure." He reached out as if to touch her before lowering his hand. For two people who had vowed to try and be friends, they were acting far too awkward for their promises to be of any consequence.

"I am. So, I guess you come here often?"

If there were a sinkhole for her to fall into, she'd look for it because, dear God, what was wrong with her?

Fox's mouth quirked into a smile, and Melody couldn't help the internal sigh at the sight of it. She must not have been getting enough sleep if just that grin put her slightly on edge. Of course, it could also be the fact that she could still feel the heat of his body against hers.

"My brother owns the place, and I try to stay in shape, so

I tend to come here instead of running outside. There's a few too many hills on the side roads for my comfort, and during tourist season, which happens to be *every* season here for some reason, there's way too many people to make jogging a thing."

Now, all she could think about was him jogging, sweating, and looking far too attractive for his own good.

"Melody?" He slid his fingers through the part of her hair that had already fallen out of its ponytail and tucked it behind her ear. She licked her lips, unable to hold back even that barest of movements at his touch.

"I should go work out. I got a membership from Loch. Sorry again for running into you." And before he could say anything else and possibly woo her into something she had already been fighting not to think about, she ran away. Okay, she didn't quite run away, but she did walk really fast to the other side of the gym where the ellipticals were located. She could feel Fox staring at her but chose to ignore it as she got on the machine and then did the silliest thing ever and waved at him, giving him a very bright smile that he would probably know was false, then went about her workout.

Fox gave her a strange look but waved back before walking out of the building. Her shoulders immediately relaxed as soon as he wasn't in her line of vision, and she forced herself to move a little faster. About ten minutes in, however, her stomach revolted, and she had to practically jump off the elliptical and search for the restroom sign. Thankfully, the door was close to her, This time, she ran.

She emptied the contents of her stomach into the bowl, her body shaking. She didn't think it was from working out. It was probably just stress. Moving to a new town, opening up her own business, and meeting her formally one-night stand all in the space of a few days would set anyone's nerves on edge.

And as she sat on the cool tile, her back resting against the stall wall as she tried to figure out if she were going to dry heave again, she really hoped that was the only reason.

Chapter 7

Fox laughed as his butt hit the ground when his nephew Nathan tackled him. Dare and Loch cracked up laughing, their bellows echoing throughout the neighborhood as Fox winced from the impact of the fall. At ten years old, Nate had grown into an amazing kid who was going through a growth spurt. He was all legs and long arms at this point, but somehow, the kid had wrangled that into a driving force into Fox's side. Of all his family, Fox had been the late bloomer, and now, watching his nephew grow up, Fox had a feeling he would be the smallest one again before too long. Nate might only be ten, but the kid was going to be a big dude, just like his dad.

"Did he hurt you?" his mom asked from the back porch as she shook her head. He could see her fighting a smile, and he couldn't help but roll his eyes as Nate stood up and held out a hand to him. Soon, Fox was on his feet and mock glaring at his mother for daring to smile or even laugh at her son's fate.

"Are you talking to me or Nate?" Fox asked, rubbing his hip.

Nate wrapped his arms around Fox's waist and grinned, a gap in his smile since he'd recently lost a tooth. How on earth had his nephew grown up so quickly? It felt like only yesterday that Nate was a little, wrapped bundle of crying and poop.

"I didn't hurt you, right?"

Fox shook his head and roughed up the kid's hair a bit. "Nope. I'm just acting like an old man since you surprised me. You're getting good at tackling."

"Uncle Loch is teaching me because of peewee. And you're not old." A wicked gleam shone in the kid's eyes, and Fox grinned. "Dad's old."

"I heard that!" Dare called out from the porch.

Fox nodded, forcing his smile back. "You know, your dad *is* old. And Uncle Loch's even older."

"Uncle Loch can kick Uncle Fox's ass, so he better watch what he's saying," Loch drawled from the porch with the rest of them.

"Language," their mother and Kenzie said at the same time, and Fox laughed out loud right along with Nate.

The two women looked at one another and starting giggling, sending the rest of the family into fits, as well. Kenzie was new to their family but had already fit in perfectly. Nate had a great mom that he lived with half the time, and Dare got Nate the other half now, but Kenzie was filling the role of stepmother with an odd ease that Fox thought perhaps surprised her. It was never easy stepping into a situation where the kid already had two loving parents who were part of his life, but Kenzie was finding her way around it and was, thankfully, friendly with Nate's mom.

Fox leaned down to tickle Nate, who ran out of his grasp so, of course, he had to try to follow the kid. Loch and Dare joined in and, soon, there were four of them rolling in the dirt and grass and trying to outdo one another.

When Fox got a kick to the ribs from Nate's foot as Loch held the kid upside down, he bent over, trying to catch his breath while the others stood back, sweaty and covered in dust and dirt.

"I think I'm too old to play like this," Fox said, winded, his voice strained from the kick.

Dare ran a hand over his jaw, wincing. "Uh, yeah, I think Loch punched something that's not going to bounce back anytime soon."

"Serves you right for playing like you're all Nate's age," their dad said from the porch before going inside. He'd grinned as he said it, so Fox had a feeling the old man wanted to join in but was smart enough not to.

"Come here, baby, let me take care of you," Kenzie said as she rushed to Dare's side before ducking under his arm and wrapping her arms around Nate in a tight hug. "How's my best boy?"

Fox and Loch cracked up. Kenzie totally fit in with their family. If their sister were living there, he had a feeling the two of them would be best friends.

"I won." Nate beamed.

"Of course, you did." She winked at Dare and wrapped her free arm around his waist, and the three of them made their way back to the house. Fox and Loch stood there, watching the new family for a bit before Loch punched him in the shoulder as brothers do.

"She's good for him," Loch said after a moment. His brother didn't speak as often as the rest of them, but when he did, it was important. If the man ever rambled, Fox always knew something was wrong—or Loch's best friend Ainsley was annoying him to no end as the two of them tended to do.

Fox agreed with his brother on how Kenzie fit in, though. She was absolutely perfect for Dare, and the two of them worked as if they had always been in each other's lives. They'd been through hell and back in order to stay together, however, and Fox was just glad they had found the happiness that had seemed to elude both of them for so long. And on the heels of that thought, for some reason, images of Melody entered his mind. He didn't know why, and it worried him now that he thought about it a little too long.

Melody was just his friend, or at least she was well on the way to becoming his friend. He hadn't texted her or called her in the past couple of days, even though he had her number now thanks to her grandmother. But after the awkward encounter at the gym, she'd been on his mind more than he cared to admit. He'd gone back over to the home she shared with her grandmother two more times to interview the famous woman who made him smile with her stories of the long-ago past, and had seen Melody both times. But he still hadn't had a full conversation with her without both of them bumbling around, trying to figure out exactly how to act around one another. It was hard to be friends when you started off by getting into each other's pants.

But even though it seemed as if it would be difficult to try and figure out how the two of them fit into each other's life, however platonic, Fox knew he was going to keep trying. Because Melody truly needed a friend, at least that's what he thought from the look in her eyes. What he should do, is introduce her to Kenzie and Ainsley because he had a feeling the three of them together could take over the entire town, but for some reason, he was being truly selfish and wanted Melody all to himself. That was probably another mistake, but he was good about making mistakes.

He and Loch walked into the home his parents had raised them in, and he couldn't help but smile at how familiar everything felt. Life might have moved along, and everyone might've grown up to start their own lives, but the feeling of home had never changed. His mother might have removed the wallpaper to paint, and his father might have built a new table for them to fit around over the years, but the sense of who they were as a family could never be redecorated out of this home.

Over the years, he had shared a room with both Dare and Loch since he was the youngest boy and his parents hadn't been sure who should get their own room since their younger sister Tabby always had her own space. So was the right of any little sister who had been forced to live with three older brothers who treated her as if she were one of their own: a girl with cooties and a baby sister to be protected all at the same time. It was no wonder she had gone to college out of state and never came back. Each of them might talk to her more than once a week on the phone, but it wasn't the same. He had a feeling he would be making another trip out to Denver soon to see her and her husband Alex before the baby came. Since they were the closest in age, he'd always felt a deep connection to his little sister.

Fox let out a sigh and shook his head as everyone started to talk around him, taking their seats at the big table where his parents had set out their family dinner. Every single time he walked into the house he had grown up in, he let his mind wander to what connections and family meant in general. Maybe it was the writer in him, but he couldn't quite get the idea of who they were as a family out of his head. According to his mother, he might be late in starting a family of his own it, but it was hard to want to start one at all when he had such a solid one to lean back on with his parents and siblings. But now, Dare and Kenzie were a unit with Nate, and Tabby and Alex were forming a family of their own all the way across the country. Somehow, he and Loch had been left behind, and he wasn't quite sure how he felt about that. And he really wasn't sure how he felt about the fact that Melody's face once again entered his mind along with that train of thought. He had slept with her once—well, three times actually—in the span of a night before she had walked out of his life for what he had thought was forever. They were just friends, or on their way to becoming friends—nothing more, nothing less. He needed to get the thought of her sweet curves and the way she had molded to him when they were pressed into one another at the gym out of his mind.

Clearing his throat, Fox strategically placed his napkin over his growing erection because every time he thought of Melody, his dick did what it wanted to. He really needed to get that reaction under control.

"Fox, did you hear me?"

He looked up at the sound of his mother's voice and blinked. "No, apparently, I didn't. Sorry, I was woolgathering. What was it that you wanted?"

His mother gave him a weird look, then smiled. "Well, Dare asked you to pass the potatoes, but Loch took care of that for you. I wanted to know what you were working on now. I know you take care of every aspect of the paper, but do you have an editorial coming up?"

This subject he could tackle easily, even if it once again reminded him of Melody. "I'm working on that article on Ms.

Pearl." He shook his head and then corrected himself. "I should say I *was* working on that article. The first part is on the site as we speak since I put it up right before I came over. The rest of the article is going in tomorrow's newspaper. If it goes well, as I hope it will, I'll be able to write more pieces on her. Her history is worth so much more than a single article."

His mom beamed. "I absolutely adore that woman. Why didn't you tell us earlier that your article had already been published? And why is it on the website before it's in print? I know I'm not a doting great-grandmother or from the Stone Age, but I still don't understand how media can work the way it does on the internet."

"Nobody really does," Fox said dryly. "And we only put up a little teaser to get people to actually read the rest tomorrow in print or on the site. They say print is dying, but in small towns like this, that's not always the case. And the paper still makes money even from the website. So don't worry that you're going to have to deal with me moving back into your basement and eating all your food."

"No, that would be Misty and me," Loch said, causing the rest of the table to laugh. Fox joined in but he couldn't help but watch his brother's face as he did so. Misty was noticeably absent at dinner, even though Loch was a single dad who never had time off from his daughter. Things had been harder when Misty was a baby and Loch had been forced to carry the infant around at all points of his job, but between school and a very understanding best friend in Ainsley—who was practically helping his brother raise the little girl, and another subject they didn't talk about—Loch was actually able to catch up on some sleep these days.

But Misty wasn't with Ainsley or any of her friends today. Instead, she was with her maternal grandparents for one of the meals that Loch had agreed to. It was awkward as hell, and Fox truly didn't know how his niece or his brother felt about the get-togethers once they were done, but it wasn't his place to question it unless someone asked for help. He knew his brother didn't like Misty not being with the Collins family, and he knew calling the relationship with Misty's maternal grandparents strained was an understatement, but there was nothing Fox could do except be there for his family if they needed him. And because he had a feeling he wasn't the only one with his mind running along those thoughts, he went back to talking about the famous Ms. Pearl.

"I don't want to tell you everything that will be in the article, but did you know the stories about how Ms. Pearl actually danced for the Rat Pack are true?"

The rest of them caught onto the conversation and asked more questions that he was deliberately coy about. He wanted his family to read his work, even if he was a little self-conscious about it. He was a writer, he had levels.

"What about her granddaughter? I know she's opening up that dance studio in town, so dancing must run in the blood."

At his mother's words, he did his best not to react. The last thing he needed was questions from his mother—or any of his family members for that matter—about why he reacted the way he did at just the mere mention of Melody.

"We didn't go into Ms. Pearl's family for this article, but if I get to do more with her, I know that's an angle we'll want to get into." That was as detailed as he could get without mentioning the fact that he had the hots for the granddaughter. Plus, he didn't know what had happened to Melody's parents, and he had a feeling that wasn't going to be an easy story.

"I'm so glad that she's opening that dance studio," Kenzie added. "I took ballet for years as a little girl but fell off the wagon. I already signed up for her barre exercises."

"And I'm excited to see you in a tutu." Dare winked, and Fox rolled his eyes.

"And Mom and Dad and Kenzie signed me up, too." Nate talked through his food before setting down his fork when his dad gave him a look. "My friend said dancing is just for girls, but Dad said those kids can go—"

Dare quickly placed his hand over his son's mouth as the rest of the table fought not to laugh. Nate had a tendency, just like his cousin Misty, to repeat every single thing the adults said.

"Dancing isn't just for girls," Kenzie put in. "There were plenty of boys in my class when I was younger. And there are even more boys now. And I know that you really love playing football, and being quick on your feet will be helpful if you want to keep being the amazing wide receiver you are."

"Misty wants to sign up too, but we haven't done it yet." Loch frowned as he said it. "She has swim team, and I know as she gets older, there will be even more teams and activities, but if she wants to try dancing, I guess I should just bite the bullet and sign her up."

Fox lifted his chin at his brother. "We'll make sure she gets to dance class on time. Between all of us, we'll make sure the kids get picked up, too. I guess that means I'll have to get better at my videography skills so I can record my best niece and nephew dancing their hearts out. And I realize that's usually the parents' job, but since I am in the media business, and the only uncle without a child of my own, I might as well give myself a role." That put a smile on his brother's face, and he knew he had said the right thing.

Until recently, Dare hadn't had the type of custody agreement with his ex that he did now. It'd been a long time coming, but Nate now lived with Dare half of the time, and that meant that Dare—and now Kenzie—could be there for things like dance practice, rather than just the performances. Loch, on the other hand, had been forced to do everything on his own, even though the rest of them had been there to try and help where they could. But his brother was proud and didn't always let others help. That had changed over time, as the reality of having a young girl to care for all on his own had settled in, but it still wasn't easy to let go of control and let his family in.

And, once again, Fox found himself the odd man out. The others started talking about what the classes would mean and how they hoped Melody would help their babies shine. He listened with half an ear, wondering how he'd gotten to the point where he was jealous that his family was starting to settle down. He was the only one without a child, but that had been true for ten years now. Well, not exactly, since Tabby didn't have children either. But now, she was pregnant, and soon, he really would be the only one without a kid. Dare and Tabby were both married, and while Loch might not be, he still had Misty in his life. All Fox had was his work and the family dinners. He wasn't quite sure how he felt about that, but he knew sitting at his family's table was probably not the best place to think about it.

Once again, he pushed those thoughts directly from his mind and sat back to relish his family. After dessert had been served, he waved off a second piece of pie since he knew he wasn't getting any younger and he didn't quite like the gym as much as his brothers did. Of course, if he could watch Melody in her very tight yoga pants and top, he might enjoy the gym a little bit more. Not that he was thinking about Melody. At all. Or ever again. Those were total lies, but he was just going to head home now and try not to think about her before he went to bed. Dreams of her had already kept him up late more than once, and jerking off to thoughts of her almost felt rude at this point.

When he found himself sitting alone on his couch holding his phone, he frowned. He wanted to text her, but he had no reason to other than to just say hi. That's what friends did, right? Friends could text out of the blue just to see how each other were doing. It wasn't as if he'd never had a friend before. But he'd never had a friend where their only connection was the fact that they had slept together. He was making things so complicated, so he growled at himself and flipped through his contacts until he found her name.

Fox: *Hi.*

He closed his eyes and groaned. Just one word. That was all he'd typed. Like a stalker. He may as well have typed something like *hey I like what you're wearing.* For a writer, he would've thought he would be able to figure out exactly what to say—or at least say something more than a single word.

Melody: *Hi there.*

The relief that floated through Fox's system was a little too much to bear, so he took a deep breath and texted again. After all, he wasn't a teenager, he could totally do this. Of course, teenagers were probably better at texting than he was, but that was another subject for another time.

Fox: *Did you have a good day? Your studio almost already?*

Melody: *It was an okay day. A lot of work online, trying to get the rosters ready and figuring out my lesson plans. It's weird to think I'm going to have lesson plans since I never thought I'd be a teacher, but here* *we are. And my studio is almost ready. Before I know it, it'll be opening day. I may just throw up again.*

Fox: *Again? Are you okay?*

Melody: *I'm fine. It's just nerves. I used to get sick before recitals when I was younger, as well. Most thought I had an eating disorder, but it was really just stress. I never had a problem with eating like some of the other girls did. And I can't believe I'm sitting here talking about throwing up and eating disorders, but here we are.*

Fox latched on to the fact that she had given him a little piece of herself and who she had been before she moved to Whiskey. He didn't like the fact that she had been sick, but he wanted to know more about her. It was probably a mistake, but he didn't care. Not right then.

Fox: *So, I know you're opening the dance studio, so I assumed you had experience. You were a dancer?*

There was such a long pause between what he had texted and her answer, he was truly afraid that he had said the wrong thing.

Melody: *I used to dance ballet and was at Juilliard for a time. But that was long ago. Now, I'm just a teacher in a small town in PA.*

He wasn't sure what he could say to that since he knew there had to be a lot of history in that one statement, but he did his best.

Fox: *There's nothing* just *about being a teacher. In fact, you'll be teaching my niece, nephew, and future sister-in-law. I'm pretty sure the family has a lot of faith in you.*

Melody: *I know you have to say that because we're friends, but thank you.*

Fox: *You know I don't have to say that.*

Melody: *Maybe.*

Fox paused as he tried to think of what to say, but then she texted again.

Melody: *Grandma showed me the article, Fox. It's…it's amazing. Thank you for doing that for her. And then I saw it mentioned online on another site, so you're making her day, week, and month right now.*

Fox frowned. Another site? That didn't make any sense, especially considering that the full article wasn't even up yet.

Fox: *I'm glad you both liked it, but what other place did you see it?*

She told him, and he froze.

Melody: *And now that I think about it, I saw it on a couple of other places on social media, too. I think you're viral, Fox. Pretty cool.*

Fox blinked, staring at his phone. Well, that was unexpected. He'd have to go and see what she was talking about because it was just an article about a fascinating woman. And it wasn't even a full story yet.

Fox: *Thanks for letting me know. Weird.*

Melody: *Well, I guess you are pretty weird, Fox. Okay, I need to go get some more work done to get ready for opening day. But thanks again for what you did for Grandma. She loves it.*

Fox: *Night-night, Melody.*

Melody: *Night, Fox.*

He stared at his phone for a second before pulling out his tablet to check the article. His eyes bugged when he saw the view numbers and clicks, and then he searched for where it had been named. A few big sites had already picked up his byline, and he had tons of emails about it—and it had only been a few hours.

Ms. Pearl, it seemed, wouldn't just be famous in Whiskey. It wasn't what Fox had planned on, but he had a feeling Ms. Pearl would have fun with it.

And as Fox leaned into the back of his couch, he had a feeling Melody would, too.

Chapter 8

Fox groaned, but it had nothing to do with feeling good. He hadn't been able to sleep the night before, and now he had dark circles under his eyes, and his body hurt because he'd worked out too hard. He would have liked to say that he'd worked out as much as he had because he wanted to get a bit stronger and bulk up to look like his brothers, but sadly, that wasn't the case.

Instead, he'd done it because he was sexually frustrated thanks to a certain blonde who had not only pressed up against him just right that day at the gym but had also been haunting his dreams even when he was awake.

This whole just staying just friends thing with Melody wasn't going to be easy, because all he wanted to do was pin her against the wall and have his way with her as she did the same with him.

He officially needed help.

He hadn't texted Melody at all the day before because he'd been trying to keep it cool even if he had no idea what he was doing. And because of that, after work, he'd done double the workout like an idiot and had ignored Loch's curious stares as sweat dripped into his eyes and his body shook with exertion.

He reasoned that if he could tire himself out, maybe he'd get rid of his hard-on and actually sleep.

It hadn't worked. Not in the slightest. And after Loch had finally kicked him out of the gym, Fox had found himself at home, exhausted, horny, and still not able to sleep.

He couldn't blame Melody for it, though. Not when he'd also been thinking about work and Ms. Pearl and all the other things he was juggling these days.

But today was his day off, and he wasn't going to think about that. Not if he could help it. That meant that he would take it easy, get some work done around the house, set up his yard for the new season, and maybe do something crazy like read a book while drinking coffee.

Unheard of for him these days.

Before he could go about his day and try to relax before another long workweek and trying to figure out his relationship with Melody, he needed to take a shower. His phone buzzed right before he headed to the bathroom.

The screen showed Melody's name, and he swallowed hard before casually answering. Or at least, what he thought was casual.

"Hey there." He cleared his throat. *Smooth, Fox. Smooth.*

"Hey. So, uh, I know I should probably call the company involved, but I don't know what to ask, and I hate sounding like a dumb blonde."

Fox grinned, not able to help himself. "You're going to have to back up a few steps. Which company? And how can I help?"

She laughed, and it went straight to his cock. Hell, he loved her laugh. "Sorry. Hi, Fox. How are you? I was in the middle of a thought when I called and, apparently, I finished my internal conversation with you instead of starting over."

"I'm just waking up. I was lazy today. Sleeping in."

"Oh! I didn't wake you?"

He shook his head, then remembered she couldn't see him. "No, I've been up, but I don't have plans today other than being lazy if I feel like it. So, what's going on, Melody?"

"Grandma Pearl wanted to watch a movie she recorded this morning, but I can't get the box to work. Now, she's off with her friends for their weekly brunch—I swear that woman has a more active social life than any teenager in Whiskey. Anyway, I'm trying to get it to work, but it keeps giving me an error message that makes no sense. I think something just needs to be rebooted, but this is a new system to me, and I could just really use any advice or help you can give me."

"Everyone in town pretty much has the same box. I can probably help you fix it rather than trying to get someone on the phone. I'll be over in a few to try and help out. Or at least help you growl at it while you fix it. That way, you're not alone." He snorted. "Technology rules our lives, and it sucks most of the time."

"Totally. You don't have to come over, but I'd appreciate it. The internet is working, same as the house phone, but the cable part isn't. Hence my anger and confusion at the damn thing."

"Give me ten minutes to hop in the shower, and I'll be over."

"Thanks," she said softly. "Sorry you're not going to have your lazy day."

"Helping a pretty woman while not having to actually work? I can still have my lazy day."

"Fox."

"What?"

"Don't call me pretty. We're not doing the flirting thing, remember?"

He pinched the bridge of his nose. It wasn't easy to remember that, but he would at least try. For her. "Got it. See you soon."

He hung up, swallowed hard, then went to take a quick, *cold* shower since he didn't need to head to Melody's with an erection from hell. It would probably all go to waste anyway since as soon as he saw her, he'd get hard all over again. But he'd at least try.

He looked down at his dick and sighed.

Okay, maybe *two* cold showers.

AS SOON AS he stepped into the big house that had always called to him, he knew that any cold showers he took when it came to Melody wouldn't help.

He was hard all over again just looking at her in her tight jeans, comfy, cotton shirt, and bare feet.

How could toes be so sexy?

"Thank you so much for coming. I actually just tried to call them to ask for help, but I ended up on like four different 'press one to enter' panels and still couldn't talk to a customer service guy. I'm so freaking annoyed. But, I made iced tea with honey. And if this doesn't work, I might add whiskey to it.

Their eyes met at the word *whiskey*, and both of them froze, their gazes locked.

He'd never look at the liquor the same way ever again. Not after her.

"Tea sounds good. Let's hold off on any *extras* until can see if I can figure anything out with your box."

He held back a cough at that, and her eyes brightened.

"Well, my *box* is over there." She winked, and his cock strained against his zipper.

He did his best not to look down below her waist at her personal *box*. Jesus, he was going to hell. But he followed her into the living room anyway, ignoring any ache down below and doing his best to forget the sexual tension burning between them.

Something he was learning he would have to get better at if he were going to survive Melody living in Whiskey.

BY THE TIME the cable box lay forgotten on the coffee table, wires and empty cups of tea next to it, two hours had passed, and Fox was ready to throw the damn thing across the room.

"It's haunted. That's the only thing I can think of." Melody sat next to him, the heat of her thigh pressed into his. His cock was beyond ready, and he had a feeling he was just going to have to get used to a perpetual state of hardness from now on.

"I cannot believe we tried fourteen things, *finally* got the place on the phone, and it's still not working." He'd lost any cred he might have had with being able to fix things. And all because of a damn cable box.

"I hate it. They may be sending a new one—which they

wanted to charge us to install. At least between us, I think we convinced them to do it for free—but they still wouldn't tell us if we lost the DVR settings or not. Grandma isn't going to be happy."

Fox reached out and squeezed her hand. "We'll figure it out."

He liked saying that. *We*. As if it were the two of them.

Friends, he reminded himself. They were *friends*.

"Thanks for everything, Fox. I guess this isn't how you wanted to spend your day."

"It's what friends do. And I had fun, even when we were yelling at the damn thing. I should go, though, since I bet you have work to do, and I promised myself I'd get my yard looking somewhat decent."

They both stood up as she smiled, and he had to do his best not to reach out and touch her. It wasn't easy, but he was stronger than the temptation. Maybe.

"I owe you one," she said softly as they walked to the front door. "Seriously."

"I'll put you to work doing yard work if you want."

She laughed again, and he took it in, the sound soothing his soul. "I don't know if I owe you that much."

They paused in the foyer, their gazes meeting, and a heated silence stretching between them.

"This doesn't count as the owing," he whispered then kissed her, knowing it was a bad idea.

He crushed his mouth to hers, her gasp lost in the kiss. Soon, her back was against the wall, his hands on her face as he deepened the kiss. He didn't touch her anywhere else, and their bodies remained a breath apart, but they were close enough that he could feel her heat.

She tasted sweet and sinful and everything he ached for.

When he pulled away, their bodies shook, and he forced himself not to kiss her again.

"That was…" she whispered.

"A mistake," he finished, not missing the hurt in her eyes. "I'm sorry. I know we're trying to be friends."

"And kissing complicates things." Her gaze met his, and he saw the need in her eyes that matched his, but he knew they both needed to take a step back if they were going to make any progress with what they had said they wanted. "I need friends, Fox. I need to be steady. You know?"

And there were no guarantees in relationships. He'd be damned if he hurt her.

"I get it. And that's why I'm going to walk out of here, and we're going to text later. Because I'm your friend, Melody. That I can promise you."

She smiled softly. "Good, because I'm your friend, too."

He respected her, and that meant he'd respect her choice. The thing was, in the end, it was his choice, too. So…no more kissing. No more thinking of her when he slept—something he wasn't sure he could control.

But he'd do his best.

Because he liked Melody, wanted her in his life. And that meant he'd take a step back and remember what they'd promised themselves and each other.

And he'd just end up sleeping with a hard dick. Again.

Chapter 9

The next morning, Melody scrolled through the news, shaking her head. There were hundreds of articles about how the world was going to end with all the pain and horrors that encroached on the lives of so many, and while Melody knew there was nothing but truth in most of those stories, she couldn't help but check out one that had nothing to do with any of that.

She knew her grandmother was an amazing woman. Even if she hadn't known some of the history behind that, she'd have figured it out. Just by being in the woman's mere presence. There was nothing usual about Grandma Pearl, and everything about the woman who shared her blood was fascinating. And Melody knew that Fox's initial story wasn't even a fraction of what had happened in her grandmother's life. Her grandma had lived a full and captivating life, and if you asked the woman, she probably would have said that she hadn't even begun living yet. And that was just one more reason why Melody wanted to be exactly like her grandmother one day.

It had been two days since the story hit the *Whiskey Chronicles* website, and she couldn't believe how many shares it already had. People were calling and sending letters already, trying to get to know the fascinating Ms. Pearl better. Melody had been busy working, trying to get everything set up for her dance studio, and she hadn't been able to figure out exactly how her grandmother felt about the new attention. If Melody hadn't been feeling so rundown from working as hard as she was, she might've been able to find the energy to prod her grandmother and figure out exactly what was going on in that head of hers.

And because Melody was working so hard, she hadn't really been able to ask Fox how he felt about it either, because they kept missing each other beyond texts. They'd tried to schedule lunch, but it hadn't happened. Other than when he'd come over to help her with her cable box—she blushed thinking about it—she hadn't seen him.

He must have been working long hours with his job, though she really didn't know what an editor and owner of a newspaper did, but adding in the extra attention his single article had been getting, she assumed he was working hours just as long as hers. She didn't know why she felt as if she were missing him, even though they'd talked over text and seen each other in person less than two days ago.

Shaking her head and trying to put thoughts of Fox's voice and the feel of him out of her mind like usual, she went to check the mail that had already come earlier that morning. Most were letters to her grandmother, bills, and junk mail. But there was one envelope addressed to her with no return address.

She frowned, wondering who on earth would be sending her a letter. Between both of her email addresses—her personal one and the one for work—she got constant electronic notes, and even texts and phone calls about the upcoming classes and from her contractor…and Fox. But she didn't know anyone besides her grandmother who would write her a letter.

She set the rest of the mail on the counter in organized piles so her grandmother wouldn't have to leaf through everything. She still didn't know what they were going to do with all the letters since it had only been two days. The people who'd written must've rushed or lived close in order to send Grandma so many, but she figured her grandmother and she would end up going through each one and making even more piles. Grandma Pearl did love her stationery and receiving letters.

When everything was organized, she set the single letter addressed to her in front of her and ran her finger over her name. She didn't know why she hesitated, but it felt weird getting something addressed to her. Fox had been very careful not to mention Melody's name or even her parents in the article. That had been something that he had told her grandmother ahead of time because they hadn't wanted to get into her family and true personal life until they were ready.

Maybe it was a letter from one of the upcoming dancers. Maybe it was a note from one of her friends from the past. That sent a chill down her spine, however. She wasn't friends with anyone from back then anymore. She had been the one to cut ties, but she knew they'd have cut them if they had the chance. She didn't deserve their friendship or their letters.

Melody closed her eyes and took a deep breath. She was once again nauseous, but this time, she had a feeling it had nothing to do with the nerves of opening a new dance studio on her own.

Swallowing hard, she flipped the envelope over and quickly opened it using one of her grandmother's fancy letter openers. Inside, there was a single sheet of paper with a handwritten note. She opened it and blinked.

Found you.

The paper fell from her fingertips, and she tried to catch her breath. Who would've sent that? Who would be looking for her? Nobody knew where she had moved to because no one was looking. And why would they say something about *finding* her? It didn't make any sense. It had to be a joke from some of the teenagers in the town or something, being weird and welcoming her. Or maybe it was someone who had figured out that she was related to Ms. Pearl and wanted to creep her out. She had no idea what it could mean, but because she had watched way too many detective shows in the past, she put the letter and envelope into a plastic bag and hurriedly hid it in the desk in her room. The letter was just a mistake. Or a joke. It meant nothing. Just like that email had meant nothing.

Her hands shook, and her stomach rolled, but she tried to push the weird feelings out of her mind. There was no cause for worry. No one was looking for her. There was no reason for anyone to look for her.

Because the people she had hurt were dead.

And the dead didn't stalk you.

Chapter 10

By the time Melody made it to her studio after hiding the letter in her desk, she was running late. It had taken her longer than she had planned to finish getting ready and get out of the house. She still couldn't quite believe that someone had sent that note, but she hoped it was just a prank. It had to be. There was no reason for her to get anything like that in the mail, and because she'd watched so many crime shows, her imagination was just running amok.

Her contractors weren't working that day because they had another project they alternated with hers. That was just fine with her, though, because she still had to set up her office and do some practice in the main room to make sure all the tiny logistics were exactly where they needed to be. She had been in countless dance studios in her life and knew what she needed as a dancer, but teaching children—or anybody for that matter—was new for her. She may have taken classes to ensure that she could do what she would be doing, but it didn't mean she would excel at it. And that meant lots of practice and making sure each piece of equipment, and the space, was perfectly attuned to what her dancers would need.

And once again, her stomach rolled, and she tried not to vomit.

She really didn't want to throw up on her new floor.

She had put on workout clothes so she could test out some of the new things her contractor had put in, so she toed off her shoes and put on an old pair of ballet flats before she started to stretch. She was nowhere near the shape she had been in in her prime thanks to everything that had happened, and there was no way she would ever be able to have that kind of endurance or stretching ability again. But she could at least do some of the initial stretches and position work to make sure that everything in the space was set up exactly like it needed to be.

And maybe she hadn't needed to follow her dreams along the path she had to this particular destination, but as her grandmother had said, there was dancing in her veins, and she had been hiding from it for far too long. There was no way she could stand alone in the stance studio for too long and not want to put her feet on every inch of the beautiful floor and let the music flow through her as she danced.

They hadn't set up the rest of the audio system yet since that was one of the last things they were going to do, so she connected her phone to the speaker and played a song that was slightly upbeat. If she had queued up anything sad right then, with all the nerves running through her, she probably would have ended up a weeping ball, never wanting to dance again.

She rolled her neck over her shoulders and held out her arms, her fingers spread ever so slightly. And then she danced. With every high and low, she moved, the music flowing through her. She didn't do any giant leaps or big spins that would end with her on pointe or on the ground, but in those moments, she was just the music, and she could feel the woman she had once been.

And because she wasn't exactly sure how she felt about that anymore, she forcibly lost herself in the music, and it took her moment to realize that someone was knocking on the door. She tripped over her own two feet, proving that being graceful didn't always come naturally, and looked out her floor-to-ceiling windows at the front the studio, trying not to fall flat on her face. Having a potential new client watch her fall on the dance floor wasn't the best way to entice people to pay for dancing lessons.

Standing at the glass double doors were two women with bright smiles on their faces. They looked sort of familiar to her, but then again, she had seen a lot of people since she'd come to Whiskey—even though she had sort of hidden herself away at her grandmother's house and at the studio. But she had a feeling she should know who these two women were.

She held up one finger, scurried back to her phone to turn down the music since it was far too loud, and did her best to look professional as she walked back to the front doors. She had locked them since she was a woman alone in an empty building, but now, she kind of felt silly dancing with the lights on where anyone could see her.

Both women smiled at her when she opened the door. "Hi there, we aren't open quite yet, but is there something I can do for you?" She used to be good at this whole people thing, or at least she had thought she was; now, she felt a little bit rusty. Considering that the only people she really talked to were her contractor, her grandmother, and Fox, she realized she really needed to get better at this whole thing.

The slightly curvier woman with the long, auburn hair gave a little wave and grinned. Melody thought *slightly* on that curvy part because they were both tall and pretty slender—and gorgeous. For a dancer, Melody had far more curves than some of her previous acquaintances. Since she wasn't dancing full-time now, she didn't mind and actually liked her curves. But if she had still been in the Juilliard world, she would've been considered fat. And she probably would've told those people to go fuck themselves and then danced her heart out. But that was neither here nor there.

The brunette waved, as well. "Hi, I'm Ainsley, and this is Kenzie. We know you've already met Kenzie's man, Dare since he owns the bar across the street. And you met his brother, Loch at the gym he owns. *And* you met Fox. We've been patiently waiting for you to come back into the bar so *we* could meet you, but we're not that patient."

Kenzie let out a laugh as Melody tried to catch up to exactly what Ainsley was trying to say. "I'm new to this whole small-town thing, too, so don't worry. Yes, the whole town knows about you and knows that you're opening a small dance studio and that a lot of us have already signed up to work with you. And the whole town is waiting for you to come out of the house and meet them so they can talk about you—but in a fun way, not a weird way. And I'm just rambling about the fact that small towns are really weird. I'm still trying to get used to the fact that everybody seems to know my name and that the only people I really know right off the bat are the others I work with and my new family. And Ainsley, of course."

"I'm practically family," Ainsley said with a laugh.

Melody was still trying to catch up when she realized that she was standing in the doorway forcing the two women to remain on the sidewalk. Now she felt awkward, but she took a step back and let them walk in anyway. She knew she had seen these two women before. Fox had pointed them out the night she wasn't ever going to mention again. Plus, he had talked about them again when they were texting each other. It was just weird to have the women in front of her and not know exactly what she was supposed to say.

"Come on in, sorry for making you wait out there. I was just stretching, getting to know the dance floor, and I think my mind is still on the music rather than how to actually have a conversation. Sorry."

"It's no worries," Kenzie said as she and Ainsley walked in, their gazes searching the place.

Melody felt a little self-conscious but she did her best not to look it. At least, she hoped she did.

"This place looks great," Kenzie continued. "I can't wait to get started. I used to dance when I was younger. I wasn't amazing or anything, but it'll be nice to have a workout that doesn't include the elliptical day in and day out. Not that I don't love Loch and his gym, but sometimes, it would be nice to do something a little different."

Melody finally caught on. "You're going to be dancing with me? That's wonderful. I wasn't actually looking at names as much as I probably should have when I was making up the rosters. I think everything is blending together at this point, and it's going to take me a few tries in order to get it."

"I run the inn and barely remember guests' names as they leave sometimes, so I totally understand. I'm just really excited that you're here."

"*We* are excited," Ainsley corrected. "I haven't signed up

for a class yet because I don't have the experience that Kenzie does. I know you have non-experienced classes, but I don't know if I'm there yet. You'll still see me around because Loch signed up his daughter Misty, and Dare signed up his son, Nate. So I will probably be here often to watch over practices and pick them up."

Melody didn't think that Ainsley was dating Loch, at least from what Fox had said, but she seemed really close to the family. There had to be a story there. Not that she was going to touch on anything close to that since it wasn't her place and she was still trying to figure out exactly how she would fit into this new town and with these new people. Digging for gossip and trying to figure out relationships was no way to go about that.

"Can I just say how excited I am that people are actually signing up? I mean, it's not like I went into opening the studio thinking I was going to be all by myself, but I totally went into it thinking I *might* be by myself, going into complete debt because I had no dancing students, and dancing alone on this floor sobbing into my ballet shoes."

The others laughed, but Melody had been totally serious, and she had a feeling the others knew that.

"Anyway, we came to say hello," Kenzie continued. "I know what it's like to be the new person in town, and this one over here completely took me under her wing so I wasn't alone. You totally don't have to become best friends with us or even hang out with us if you don't want. But I wanted to let you know that we're here if you need a set of girlfriends."

Melody couldn't help but smile. She'd never met women like these two before, and she knew she'd been sorely missing out. Her past friends had been just as cutthroat as she was, and she regretted what had become of everything.

"And I'm going to be blunt and say that I want to know exactly what you were doing that night with our dear Fox." Ainsley looked like she was a cat in cream, and Melody just stood there blinking.

"What?"

"What Ainsley is trying to say, is that we remember you doing shots of whiskey with Fox one night a little over three months ago. However, we are not going to talk about that right now because it is totally none of our business. Right, Ainsley? Did we not just have this discussion and say we weren't going to mention the fact that we know the two of them left one night completely wasted? The guys didn't notice, but we did. But don't worry, Melody. We're not going to talk about this ever again. Right, Ainsley?"

"Oh dear God. I didn't think anyone had noticed. Oh my God. This whole move just got really complicated, really fast." Melody had no idea what she was going to do with this information. She had been doing her best not to think about the fact that she had slept with Fox and had the best sex of her life with him. And then she tried not to think about the fact that she really wanted to have sex with him again, and that they had both decided they wouldn't because they were trying to be friends. She'd moved to this small town to find friends and a new life, and now…things had gotten really complicated, and she was just so freaking embarrassed.

"Since you're talking about it, can we?" Ainsley asked, a curious look on her face. Melody had a feeling she was trying to look innocent but there was nothing innocent about this woman in front of her. At least, not yet.

"Ainsley," Kenzie laughed.

"What?"

"Okay, I will say this just once. So that it's out in the open and we can forget that I ever said it at all. Yes, Fox and I had sex. I didn't realize he actually lived here until I was too drunk to care. Yes, we had sex. Yes, we've talked about it. No, we aren't going to do it again. Yes, we are going to be friends. Yes, it is awkward, and I have no idea what I'm doing. And I have no idea why I'm saying all this out loud to you. But, apparently, it has been bursting inside of me, and I couldn't wait to tell *somebody*, so I had to tell the two people who I just met about thirty seconds ago. Now excuse me while I go find a hole to bury myself in. I will talk to you later."

The other two laughed, and Melody seriously needed to find that hole. Why was it never handy when she needed it?

"Fox is sexy, just not as sexy as my Dare."

"*So* not having this conversation," Melody said, laughing. "I really cannot believe I just put all of that out there like that."

Ainsley studied her face. "So you two had sex. And it was probably amazing because you're blushing and you aren't looking like you're grossed out. And considering he's a Collins brother, I can assume that's a pretty good guess." She paused. "Not that I know what sex is like with one of them, but I hear things."

"I don't think I'm going to answer that," Melody said with a laugh. "Not that it was a question, but I'm so not going to answer that."

Kenzie just shook her head, her smile widening. "Okay, enough of that. We'll just get you tipsy one day so you spill everything. But, really, if you need friends, we're here. I really do know what it's like to move to a new place and not know your way around. In fact, if you want to join us for lunch, we're heading to Dare's since I'm addicted to his new tomato grilled cheese."

Melody's stomach normally would have rumbled just then, but she blinked, her head going a bit fuzzy as her stomach rolled instead.

"Melody?" Ainsley asked, her voice sharp.

Instead of answering, Melody tried to take a step forward, but her body felt suddenly heavy. The others said her name, but she felt as if she were walking through fog. Hands wrapped around her arms, and she suddenly felt herself being lowered to the ground, though she couldn't really focus. Instead, black dots danced around her eyes just as she had been dancing around the floor, and then there was nothing. Only silence.

MELODY WOKE up only a few moments later, but by then, she was lying on the floor, her head resting on Kenzie's lap as Ainsley talked on the phone to whom she assumed was the paramedics. She had tried to wave off her new friends, saying that it must just be a stomachache and spinning around too much. But even she didn't quite believe that.

And that was how she found herself sitting alone in a hospital room after somehow making the other women not call an ambulance to pick her up. They had demanded to take her to the doctor themselves, however. Melody had kept putting off getting a new primary care physician, and she knew why she was afraid of going to the doctor, but she couldn't keep running anymore. She had seen enough of the inside of hospital rooms in her lifetime, and now it seemed she was right back in one.

The doctor had been nice enough, and the nurse had taken a blood sample because Melody had been so lightheaded. Ainsley and Kenzie were in the waiting room, and Melody had a feeling if she hadn't put her foot down, they would be right in her hospital room beside her.

She was fine, everything was fine. It was just nerves.

The door opened, and a nice, elderly doctor walked in, a calm smile on his face.

"I skipped breakfast, and I think my blood sugar is just low. That's it, right? I'll do better about eating. I know that I need to eat breakfast. I just forgot today."

He set down her file, and she noticed a prescription written out on top, but she couldn't read what it was for. She hated pills, and she really hoped that everything was okay.

"You really do need to eat breakfast, Ms. Waters. And that is something we can talk about in the future, as well. But your blood tests came back quickly since we put a rush on them. The results mean that you're *really* going to need to keep eating. Because you're not just eating for yourself anymore. Melody, you're pregnant."

She blinked. She had to have heard him wrong. Because there was no way she could be pregnant. She hadn't had sex in over three months, and even then, they had used a condom. Three condoms, one for each time they had sex. And birth control. There was no way there could be a little baby growing inside her stomach right then. Because she was about to open a dance studio. And she couldn't do that if she were pregnant. And it wasn't as if she were seeing anyone. The test had to be wrong. When she tried to explain all of that to the doctor in one rushed sentence, she swore she saw a pitying look in his eyes.

"We can and will run the test again, but you're pregnant, Melody. And if you say you haven't had sex in over three months, then you're a little over three months along. I'm going to refer you to the best OB/GYN in our town, and they'll be able to set up an appointment to discuss exactly what you want to do."

She swallowed hard, her hands shaking. "I can't be pregnant. I mean, my periods have always been horrendously irregular because of genetics and the fact that I was a dancer for so long. And that's just what happens to us. So I didn't even think about the fact that I haven't had them. But, it doesn't make any sense. This can't be happening."

And as the doctor kept speaking, telling her about prenatal vitamins and the appointment she could make with the OB/GYN and the options she had, she kept all of that in the back of her mind as all she could focus on was the fact that, somehow, she and Fox had created a baby.

She would have to tell him.

And she really had no idea what she was going to do.

She had known that whiskey-induced night would change things; she just hadn't realized how much. Until now.

She was screwed.

Chapter 11

Fox leaned against the office wall in the back of Dare's bar, juggling three lemons. Dare hated when he did this, but Fox needed to think. He had another story brewing in the back of his mind, even as he worked on a hundred other things having to do with the paper. Plus, by the success of his first article with Ms. Pearl, he knew he needed to do at least one more. It was all up to what she wanted to do, rather than what he needed to do.

Unlike some reporters, he knew that Ms. Pearl was the most important part of the story, and that meant if she didn't want to do a follow-up, he wouldn't. And though she had wanted him to come over tonight to talk more and see where the story would go, nothing was set in stone.

She never wanted to be part of the big papers and the heartbreaking news so often found in them, and that had never been part of his life. He liked what he did, and he didn't know if he liked the fact that so many people were contacting him now that they'd gotten to know the woman who knew the famous people back in the day. He knew his town would keep Ms. Pearl safe, and he wasn't really worried about that, but it still felt weird to have so many more eyes on his work than usual.

He really was weird, even for a writer.

And because his phone wouldn't stop ringing at work, he had tasked his assistant with dealing with all of that, and the rest of his employees were either off working on their own stories or doing research, so he was sitting in his brother's office, avoiding work rather than even helping out at the bar. It wasn't yet dinnertime, so it wasn't as if Fox's help was needed, but he really was just avoiding everything.

"I really wish you would stop stealing the produce," Dare said as he walked back into his office, yet another folder of paperwork in his hand. Fox thought he had to deal with enough paperwork with his own job, but both of his brothers had even more than he did most days. How all three ended up owning their own businesses, he had no idea. It wasn't what his brothers had grown up thinking they would do. But, here they were. And if he were honest with himself, their sister had even more paperwork than the rest of them combined. She practically ran a huge business out in Colorado with her husband and his family.

"I'd make a joke about life giving me lemons or something, but I really don't know where I would go with that."

"Please don't make a joke. I have a headache since both of my waitresses are working their assess off, and yet we're getting too busy for just the two of them. We're probably going to have to hire a third waitress or pull someone over from the restaurant side and make everybody stressed out. I think I can get Kenzie to work tonight along with me, but she's already been working all day at the inn, and now I'm just going to have a bigger headache, and my girl is going to be exhausted."

"I have a meeting with Ms. Pearl later, but after that, I can probably come in and help. I would cancel on her, but no one really cancels on Ms. Pearl."

"Duly noted, and I thank you in advance. And yeah, do not cancel on Ms. Pearl. And I didn't tell you this before, but great job on that article. Really good stuff." Dare's head was down as he searched through paperwork but Fox knew that his brother was sincere.

It had been a really good story, after all.

"I talked with Tabby earlier, and she said that she's probably going to call later tonight. You might want to text her and tell her you'll talk to her tomorrow if you'll be in the bar all night working since we're short-staffed. I like that she's been calling more often since the wedding and now news of the baby, but I also hate the fact that it just reminds me that our baby sister is so far away. Now, she's going to be a mom herself, and the baby will be a Montgomery, and all those Montgomerys just keep breeding so she will end up with like eighteen children by the time we get to see her again."

Dare looked over his shoulder and smiled. "I don't really think that's how the whole pregnancy thing works. But it's been a long time since Nate was born so I could be wrong."

Fox laughed and stopped juggling since he could see it was getting on Dare's nerves. He might be the little brother, but he'd long since given up the notion that his sole role in life was to annoy his two older siblings. Most of the time anyway.

"You and Kenzie thinking about having babies of your own soon? Or if that's not a question I should ask right now, you can just look away and go back to your paperwork."

Dare turned and leaned against his desk, folding his arms

over his chest. "We're trying. I don't know if I was supposed to tell you that or not, but our family apparently tells each other everything these days, so…yeah. We're trying. Kenzie's afraid that she's getting too old to start thinking about having babies, even though she's not even thirty yet and it's not like she's in that window. But we kind of want to give Nate more than one younger sibling, so that means we have to start trying earlier rather than later. And, yeah, we're not married yet, but we like to do things backwards. It's just how we are. But she's my life. She is going to be it for me. So that means I get to start trying to make a baby with the person I love most in the world, I count that as a win. By the way, the whole marriage thing? I'm working on it. We both said we wanted to wait until we at least hit six months together, but I don't know if we'll wait that long. Knowing Kenzie, she'll be the one to propose to me."

Fox smiled widely, thinking about Kenzie going down on one knee for Dare and then the two raising even more kids. "The idea of you and Kenzie having kids is possibly the best thing I've heard all day. Thank God Kenzie is hot because Nate is a cute kid, but it all comes from his mom. Not your ugly mug."

"You're lucky we're at work, or I'd kick your ass right now." Dare shook his head, glaring at his papers. "And, once again, I don't get why you're here instead of in your office."

"I think better in yours."

"That makes no sense. My office is tiny and cramped and smells like fried food and beer, even though Kenzie and I have repeatedly tried to change that. And your office has actual windows that air out the place as much as you want. Plus, you never have family members frolicking inside because they like your office better."

Fox set the lemons down on Dare's desk and glared. "I did not, nor have I ever, frolicked."

"I'm just calling it like I see it." Dare's eyes filled with laughter, but Fox didn't reach out and punch his brother like he wanted to. Somehow, Kenzie or even their parents would show up just at that moment and scold them, and he'd been in trouble. He supposed the two of them—no, *three* since Loch was just as bad as they were—needed to grow up at some point.

"You're cruel. And on that note, I need to head to Ms. Pearl's. I'll be back later though to help behind the bar."

Dare nodded, his attention on his books again. "Thanks. I know you don't have to help, but I appreciate it."

Fox squeezed his brother's shoulder on the way out the door. "You let me use your office and bar to work when I need space to think and write, and if I were the one who owned this place, you'd help out the moment I needed it—and probably before since you'd realize I needed the help. We're family. It's what we do."

And on that note, Fox headed out before they got too into their feelings, and he ended up making Dare uncomfortable. His brother was getting better since he'd gotten with Kenzie, but there were still some things Dare didn't like to talk about. Loch was even worse, and it made Fox realize why he and Tabby were so close—because Fox actually told people what he was feeling. Maybe it was the writer in him, maybe it was because he and his sister were closest in age and she never let him get away with anything. But he at least tried to be transparent.

At least until it came to Melody.

Because hell if he knew what he was doing there.

And now that he was headed to Ms. Pearl's, he knew

there was a high probability that he'd see Melody at the house. He knew Kenzie and Ainsley had been planning to stop by her studio since he'd asked them if they'd met her yet. He'd ignored their all-too-knowing looks because he'd known that Melody would need more friends than just him in this town if their hormones didn't calm down soon. However, he had no idea if the two had actually made it to the studio or what had happened. He figured if he saw Melody, he'd find out tonight, or maybe he'd text her. And if he were too chicken to do that, he'd just ask Kenzie and Ainsley.

Melody affected him to the point where he kept second-guessing all his decisions, and he didn't know what that meant other than he was pretty sure he wanted to see her again—and not just as friends. But they'd agreed to be *just* friends, so now he had no idea what he was doing. Yes, they'd kissed when they shouldn't have, but they'd reaffirmed to each other that they needed to remain friends in order to stay steady. Or whatever that meant.

Tonight, though, was about work, and he'd just have to suck it up and stop thinking about Melody naked—or in his life in any way but as friends.

Totally easier said than done since he couldn't get the thought of Melody and her rosy nipples out of his mind.

"And that's enough of that," he growled as he got into his car and drove toward Ms. Pearl's place. It had been raining on and off all day, so he'd driven instead of walked so he wouldn't get his work wet. He'd need to head into the gym soon too since he hadn't been walking the town as much as usual. Of course, as soon he thought about the gym, he thought about Melody and her body pressed close to his.

He needed to get her out of his system, or he would end up insane.

Grumbling, he parked in front of the house and made his way up to the front door. It was just starting to drizzle again, so he was glad that when he knocked, someone answered right away. Melody stood on the other side, her face pale and her body wrapped in a blanket.

Fox immediately let himself inside and cupped her face. "What's wrong? Are you okay? You should be sitting down, not answering the door."

She shrugged, pulling away from him. "Just a weird day," she said, her eyes not meeting his. "And someone had to answer the door, or you'd be standing on the porch in the rain the whole time. Grandma is sleeping upstairs. She had a headache." She paused. "Were you supposed to meet her tonight? I didn't know, or I'd have texted you. I'm sorry you came all the way out here for nothing."

Worried, he tugged on her hand and led her into the living room. "Sit. And don't worry about not texting me. If your grandma has a headache, of course she should be napping. I'm just sorry neither of you is feeling well."

She tilted her head, studying him. "I'm not feeling well?"

"You're wrapped in a blanket and pale. I assumed. Now sit down because you're worrying me." He pressed down on her shoulders, and she sank onto the couch. The fact that she did it so easily worried him.

"I'm fine." But as she said it, she rested her head on the back of the couch and closed her eyes. "Really. I'll be fine."

He knelt down in front of her, taking her hand. "If your grandma has a headache and is upstairs, who is taking care of you?"

"I don't need to be taken care of." She opened her eyes, giving him a small smile that almost reached her eyes. "I'm just a little tired. Long day, you know." She searched his face, and he tilted his head, studying hers in turn. "You didn't talk to the girls, then?"

He blinked. "The girls?" He felt as if he were missing something; two steps behind. But when it came to Melody, he usually felt like that.

She cleared her throat, looking distinctly uncomfortable. "Ainsley and Kenzie stopped by the studio today. They were nice." She paused. "I remember them from that night." Her cheeks finally held a little bit of color, and he relaxed somewhat.

"I didn't know they'd stopped by, but they did mention that they wanted to. Kenzie is pretty new to town, as well, so they wanted to make sure you had a support system if you needed one."

"They were nice. They seemed nice that night, too. Though I guess we didn't really get to talk with them, did we?" She cleared her throat again, her gaze darting from his, and he couldn't help but lean forward and trace his thumb along her jaw. He didn't know what it was about her, but he couldn't keep his hands off of her. And if it weren't for the fact that her fingers were slowly tracing his other arm at that exact moment, he might've felt a little bad about it. They were not doing this friendship thing the way they probably should, but it wasn't as if he knew what he was doing.

He'd never tried to be friends with a woman after he slept with her. That made him sound like an asshole. His relationships just hadn't ended up where he and his partner could be friends. Every single one had either not been serious enough, or they had drifted apart to the point where he was no longer in their lives. Melody seemed to be the exception, and he wasn't quite sure what that meant.

And because he wasn't sure, he knew that what he was about to do was beyond stupid.

Her face had colored again, and she no longer looked like she had when he first walked into the house. She licked her lips, and his gaze couldn't help but drift down at the motion, her tongue peeking out once again. His thumb grazed her chin again, and he slowly slid his hand around to the back of her head, his fingers tangling in her hair.

The tips of her fingers kept playing with his other forearm, and he let out a shaky breath before he leaned forward and pressed his lips to hers. He knew this was a mistake. They were supposed to be friends. Only friends. Friends where they both knew the need was too much, too intoxicating.

And, hell, he'd just told her that he wanted her to sit down because she looked pale?

He was such a damn lecher.

Fox pulled away and rested his forehead on hers, knowing that if he looked into her eyes now and saw disgust or shame, he would never forgive himself. He hadn't meant to kiss her. Hell, he had only meant to come to this house to work and perhaps try and keep his friendship with Melody healthy. Instead, all he had done was worry, and now kiss her when he knew he shouldn't.

Melody did something to him, but there was no blame on her shoulders, there never could be.

He was the one who needed to find his control, because she had said she was too overwhelmed to think about a relationship, and their being together one night didn't constitute a commitment beyond that single moment. And that was something he would just have to remember.

He was just about to pull away when something wet

touched his thumb. He pulled back, shocked. Tears streaked down her face, and his stomach rolled. What had he done?

"Melody? What's wrong? Oh, God, did I hurt you? I shouldn't have kissed you like that. It was wrong of me, and I told myself it was a mistake, but I couldn't stop from kissing you just then. I'm so sorry that I hurt you. I can leave right now if you need me to. Leave and never come back. I promise. Just please don't cry."

Melody mumbled something under her breath, but he didn't quite catch it. He didn't reach out and wipe her tears away, and he did his best not to touch her at all. He'd kissed her, and now she cried. He was a damn fool and deserved whatever lashing she gave him."

"Talk to me. Or don't. If you want me to leave, I can do that, too. I just don't want to leave you like this, Melody. Not if I can help it."

"I'm pregnant."

He blinked, not quite understanding what she had just said. But even though he couldn't comprehend the words, his mouth went dry, and his body went as still as a statue.

"What?"

Melody looked at him for a moment then lowered her head, her gaze on her hands. And then she pretty much broke down.

"I'm pregnant. Oh, God. I hate whiskey. Whiskey is evil. Whiskey and everything named whiskey. Why did this happen? How could this happen? Whiskey is the devil, and so are the brothers who own a damn whiskey bar." She looked up then, her eyes wide with panic he had never seen before. "Oh my God, my baby is going to be named Whiskey. It's all on the damn whiskey. All the blame."

He patted her hand as if he thought that might comfort

her as he tried to get his thoughts in order. She was pregnant? As in, a baby coming in nine months or he guessed less than that since she kept talking about whiskey. He swallowed hard and found that his mouth was too dry for even that to work, and so he just sat there, blinking.

"That was a lot of whiskey." Okay, he probably could've said something a little more helpful, but even as a writer, he was at a loss for words.

"I know it was partly the whiskey," Melody said quickly. "That's why we're in this situation."

"We. You mean *we*. As in you and me. As in that one night a little over three months ago when we had all that whiskey? We also made a baby? But we used a condom. Lots of condoms. Birth control. We were safe. We were really, really safe. I mean, we were drunk, but we were safe. But you're saying that you're pregnant, and now the whole you being pale and looking shell-shocked thing makes sense. Because you wouldn't have just blurted it out like that or look like you're ready to vomit if you weren't pregnant. Oh, God, I think I need to sit down."

"You are sitting down." Melody reached out and patted his hand, and he looked down to notice that, yes, he was indeed sitting on the floor and no longer kneeling in front of her. Somehow, in all of his panic, Melody's breaths had started to slow down, and she looked the calm one of the two of them. Fox was usually the calm one—not as serene as Loch, but…enough. And now he was sitting here letting his mind go in a thousand different directions, and he had no idea what he was doing.

Pregnant.

How the hell did that happen?

"Pretty much how it always happens."

He hadn't realized he'd said that out loud until she answered. "I mean, I know how it happens. I remember everything about that night, too. We may have been drunk, but that was the best sex of my life, and now it seems that sex had consequences. Hell, sex always has consequences but they don't always have to do with babies or STDs. And why the hell am I talking about STDs and sitting on the floor away from the woman who is carrying my child?"

Melody laughed. This time, the tears streaming down her face didn't make him want to hurt whoever had dared to hurt her. But the fact that he had been the one to make her cry wasn't lost on him.

"I'm glad to see that you're panicking, too. Because that whole thing where I talked about whiskey and that I think the baby should be named Whiskey…that was like my fifth panic attack in the past few hours. Good to know we are both on the same page of not knowing what the hell is going on. And I just keep rambling."

Fox sucked in a deep breath and tried to calm his erratic heartbeat. "Okay. We're both panicking, so I guess I should try to calm down so I can figure out what's going on. Because I feel like my brain is like five steps behind reality, and it keeps thinking stupid shit that might not be funny once we actually think about it for real."

"I know what you mean. I keep going through random bouts of giggling, and then crying jags, and then just sitting as if I know what to do next. Yet I'm still nauseous at the same time."

That made Fox sit up straighter. "Nauseous? Are you okay? You need water or peanut butter? I've no idea if the pregnancy myths are true or when they even start. And by *they*, I mean cravings. I should just shut up now."

Melody reached out and cupped his face. Her soft hand on his slightly scratchy cheek calmed him more than anything else could have.

"I'm fine. Or at least I will be fine. Let's talk about the details so that way we can figure out exactly what to do because you may feel ten steps behind, but I'm right there with you."

"Okay. I can do that."

"Good. I didn't realize I was pregnant until today. I know that sounds stupid, considering how far along I am but, apparently, it's more common than we think. This is probably too much information, but I don't really care because, hello, I'm having a baby and I'm stressed out. I don't usually get my period regularly, so I can't use that as a timeframe. I'm fine, but it has to do with my dancing when I was younger. So because I didn't realize I had missed any periods, I wasn't looking for any other symptoms. I also thought that the nausea and the times when my stomach rolled had to do with the stress of moving to a new town, opening up a new business, becoming friends with you… I didn't realize it was morning sickness until today."

She took a deep breath, but he didn't interrupt her because he had a feeling she wasn't finished yet.

"I got really lightheaded today and passed out. Only for a moment. I'm fine, but I did it in front of Kenzie and Ainsley, and they made sure I made it to the doctor's. I had thought they might've told you that I passed out because I don't know exactly how small towns work, but I'm also not sure if they know exactly what happened. Now I'm getting away from the point, so I'm going back. I passed out. Not because I'm sick, not because of not taking care of myself, but because I'm pregnant, and I just got a little lightheaded. I'm going to take my vitamins, I'm going to eat better, and then I'll figure out what the hell I'm going to do because I'm over three months along now, and I'm really, really scared."

Nothing else she could have said would have hit him harder than that. He immediately stood up so he could sit on the couch and then pulled her into his arms and onto his lap. He almost thought he'd made another mistake until she leaned into his hold and clung to him.

Fox had no idea what they were going to do. He didn't question if he was the father, didn't wonder if she was pregnant at all. Because that's not who he was, and while he didn't know every aspect of Melody, he knew that wasn't who she was either.

"We'll figure it out. We'll figure it out." Maybe if he said it a few more times, he might actually believe it. Because as he sat on the couch and held Melody close, his mind whirled, and he tried to catch his breath.

Melody was pregnant. The baby was his.

He was going to be a father.

What the hell were they going to do?

Chapter 12

Today would be a better day. And if Melody kept telling herself that, it would totally happen. She wasn't going to throw up, pass out, or cry in Fox's arms. She had done enough of that the day before, and she was over being a drama queen. She had spent way too many years of her life being that person and overreacting to every single little thing because her life had been all about dance. Nothing else mattered. But she was not going to allow herself to regress.

"Easier said than done," she whispered to herself.

She stood in front of the long mirror in the room her grandmother had let her have, trying not to let her stomach roll any more than it already was. She wasn't showing yet, and she had no idea when she would start. She was months behind where she needed to be, weeks behind reading and checking on websites and making sure she could be a good mom.

And what struck her the most out of all of that, was that

in the day she had known she was pregnant, she hadn't once thought about *not* having the baby. The doctor had said she was pregnant, and even though it hadn't quite sunk in yet, her thoughts had gone to how to tell Fox and what she was going to do as a mom.

Other things like how to tell her grandmother, and how the hell she planned to run a dance studio while she was pregnant also filled her mind, but not having the baby had never been an option.

And if she were honest with herself, Fox's reaction had been something of a revelation, as well. He hadn't questioned paternity. Hadn't even doubted that she was pregnant at all. He had just sat there, rambled right along with her, and had said that they would form a plan. Neither of them had been up to actually forming a plan then, but saying something along those lines had at least calmed her enough to think that they could figure this out.

And because she felt as if she *were* calm about it, she knew it hadn't quite hit her yet. She'd had less than twenty-four hours for her mind to go through everything that she needed to go through, and all she could think about was that she really needed a nap. That and the fact that Fox had been wonderful. Yeah, he'd fallen on his ass in front of the coffee table and had mumbled and rambled just like she had, but there hadn't been a Fox-shaped hole in the door from him running away.

He had stayed. He believed her. And, somehow, she felt as if he believed *in* her.

Only her grandmother had ever truly believed in her—even those times when she didn't believe in herself. And the fact that Fox had just shakingly held her, confused her more than anything.

She didn't really want to analyze those thoughts, though. She hadn't been lying when she told Fox before all of this happened that she didn't want to deal with a relationship. She truly didn't want to open herself up to anything like that again and risk getting hurt. But she knew it was more than that. Because if she focused on what she could have been she would mess up what she'd already worked towards.

But it seemed that all of that might've gone out the window with one whiskey-filled night.

All of her plans about forming this new life of hers where it would center on her work and caring for her grandmother felt as if they were sliding through her fingers. She had no idea how she was going to juggle everything. No idea how she was going to handle being pregnant at all. And just using that word, *pregnant*, made her hands shake and her stomach roll once again. She honestly didn't know if the nausea came from morning sickness or from the idea that she knew she was pregnant.

This was such a new experience for her, and she was truly afraid that though she had tried so hard not to end up alone as she had been for so long, she feared she would end up doing this alone anyway.

She wasn't going to put any excess baggage on her grandmother. Grandma Pearl was a force to be reckoned with and had lived her life hard and strong and to its fullest. Melody didn't want to take away any of the time her grandmother had left, or fill it with worry and stress over what Melody was doing with *her* life.

She'd already done enough of that as it was.

In the end, Fox had held her and told her that everything was going to be okay and that they would figure something out. How could she believe that? She didn't know him. Yet she'd let herself fall into his arms not once, but twice now.

She hadn't forgotten that kiss either.

It had convinced her to tell him exactly what was on her mind. She hadn't known how she was going to break the news to him; how she would tell him that she was carrying his child. Yet with one kiss, she had been lost. But with Fox, that wasn't anything new.

After all, a single kiss was how they'd gotten into their situation to begin with.

And though he seemed as if he were going to be by her side, how could she trust that? How could she put Fox through that? He had his life in order. He looked as if he knew exactly what he was doing in the small town with his family surrounding him. And now she felt as if she were stripping all that away because of the one night they had spent together. This child might be both of their responsibilities, but she still didn't have any of the answers.

She was once again working herself up into circular reasoning in an argument that made no sense. So she rested her hand on her belly, the awe sliding through her at what she held shocking, and let out a deep breath.

"Now or never." Since the contractors were working on the studio today and her grandma had plans with friends, she was headed over to Fox's to talk. He had said that he was going to take the day off from work, though she wasn't quite sure how he'd do that since he owned the paper. But since that's what he had said, she was just going with it.

However, the idea of talking with Fox worried her. Maybe *worried* wasn't the best word for it, but she was still nervous. She had no idea what he would say, and she had even less idea what she was going to say. Because even though a small part of her wanted to tell him that he didn't have to take any responsibility and that she could do it on her own, the rest of her knew that was totally not the case.

She did not want to do this alone.

But she had a feeling this small town and Fox's family within its borders wouldn't allow that to happen anyway. Now there was that nauseous feeling once again. She was going to be that woman. Yes, *that* woman. The one who slept with one of Whiskey's most eligible bachelors and ended up pregnant.

Accidental pregnancies were not supposed to happen in this century, yet her body did not agree. And that was enough of that.

Melody grabbed her purse, left a note for her grandmother telling her where she was headed, and knowing there would probably be questions later, she headed out so she could walk to Fox's place. His house wasn't too far away, and she needed the air. As she made her way to the front of his home, she couldn't help but remember the first time she had been there. He'd been so caring with her, so sweet, even as he'd let her ride him into oblivion. It had been hard, fast, and hot. He'd said it was the best sex of his life, and she knew it was the same for her. She'd never had anything like it, and knew she probably never would again. No man could ever live up to Fox, and that should have scared her, but for some reason, it didn't.

But she had too much on her mind to worry about that strange thought.

Fox opened the door before she even had a chance to knock and gestured her inside. He looked far too good in worn jeans and a Henley. The fact that he wore no shoes so she could see his feet should have grossed her out, but she was a ballet dancer and had seen way worse feet. And if she were honest, Fox's feet were hot.

And that's when she knew that there was something off with her body chemistry because she had thoughts like those running through her mind. Maybe all pregnant ladies had weird kinks. Or maybe every single part of Fox was hot, and she just needed to get over herself. Finding the father of your unborn child attractive shouldn't be weird, but Melody was anything but normal.

"You came."

At Fox's words, she turned to look at him and frowned. "Of course, I came. We both said that we needed to talk since we each took the morning off. So, here I am. Did you think I would run away?" The thought had crossed her mind more than once, but running away from her problems hadn't helped before, and she knew it sure as hell wouldn't help now.

Fox shook his head and closed the door behind him. Then he reached out and gripped her hand with his. Because she was so off-kilter, so touch-starved, she let him.

"No, I didn't think you would run away. But a small part of me thought everything that happened last night was a weird dream that I couldn't quite wake up from. But now that you're here, and we're both acting so strange, I have a feeling I didn't dream up anything."

Melody barely resisted the urge to rest her hand on her nonexistent bump. She never used to do that at all before yesterday, and yet she had done it twice already that morning. Apparently, knowing there was a baby growing inside you turned you protective and gave you the same gestures that every pregnant woman and every TV show she'd ever watched had.

"Nope. Not a dream. I threw up this morning I think to remind myself exactly what happened."

Fox's face went slightly pale, and he reached out for her before lowering his arm. The two of them truly had no idea what they were doing, and it made their interaction awkward.

"Is there anything you need? I stayed up most of the night and read a bunch of articles. I even downloaded that *What To Expect* book, but I got confused and figured that was something maybe we should read together. Or maybe you already read it. But then I realized that you've only known about this a few hours longer than I have, so you probably haven't read the book yet. I don't actually know your reading speed because I don't know anything about you beyond how you taste…and that was awkward as hell, so I am going to shut up now. Wait, I'm not going to shut up. I meant to ask you if you needed anything to drink or to eat or to sit down or if there's anything I can do for you at all. And, once again, I'm going to shut up."

If Melody weren't already sure she'd been slowly falling for Fox since the night they met, she'd have known right then. He was just so damn caring, so *perfectly* imperfect and awkward.

She was just the same, and she had a feeling they would both be rambling their way into uncomfortable situations more than once as they tried to figure out what they were going to do about the whole *baby* thing.

Because, dear God, they were having a baby.

A real baby.

A baby that was currently inside her like that thing from *Alien*.

Fox's hands gripped her upper arms, and she blinked so

his face came into focus. "You just got really pale. What's wrong?"

Was it wrong of her that she wanted to lie and say that she was pale because she thought she might be falling in love with him rather than mentioning the fact that she couldn't get that horrible scene from *Alien* out of her head?

She'd officially lost her damn mind, but she told him the truth anyway. Just not about the love thing because that was something she was pretty sure she would have to hide away forever if she wanted to stay sane.

"I was just thinking about the fact that when my stomach rolls now, I don't know if it's nausea or the thing from *Alien* trying to escape. And that probably puts me in the record books for being a bad mother, but I've only been at this gig for about twenty-two hours now, so hopefully, you'll let that slide."

Fox stared at her for a moment, and she thought he might say something that would make her feel like an idiot, but he threw back his head and laughed.

"Oh, God. I'm so glad you said that because I totally had that image in my brain when you were talking about this yesterday. But I didn't want to say it because it sounded so insensitive and insane. But if you're thinking it and I'm thinking it, then it has to be okay. And that means we are totally in this together because we've lost our minds."

She shook her head, a smile playing on her lips. "I don't really know if the basis for good parenting should be a shared imagination of an alien ripping through stomach lining and murdering people in a hospital room. But it has been a while since I've seen the movie so I could be wrong about the mothering instincts of extraterrestrials."

That sent both of them into a fit of laughter, and soon,

she found herself in Fox's arms as he held her close, rubbing his hands down her back. And though she knew it was meant to be comforting, she couldn't help but inhale his scent and remember how he felt when he hovered over her that night.

"I didn't even ask you what you wanted to do with the baby. I know I should have. And I know it's your choice and understand I'll be here, no matter what happens. But I want you to know that even if you decide that you never want to talk to me again, I'm not really going away. Because, yeah, my mind is whirling and I still feel like I'm two steps behind, but I'm going to be there for you and the baby. And I'm not going to be there with just a paycheck. I know you don't really know anything about my family, and that is something that's going to change soon I think, but I have watched both of my brothers deal with being some variation of single fathers. I've watched what happens when custody agreements pull children away from their dads, even if it sounded like a reasonable explanation at the time. And I've watched my eldest brother raise his daughter on his own because his ex wanted absolutely nothing to do with being a mom. I don't want that for whatever child we have. I've watched my family struggle, and I've watched those children thrive, and I've tried to be the best uncle that I can be. But I want you to know that I want to be the man you need me to be, in any way you need it. But I don't want to just be a figment of this child's life. So, if you choose to continue on with this pregnancy, I hope you let me be by your side. I hope that you let me figure out how to be part of this child's life."

He swallowed hard, and Melody tried to figure out the words that she needed to say because she was so overwhelmed with emotion she could barely catch her breath.

"That was a lot more than I had planned to say while

standing here holding you in the front part of my house. I haven't even let us into the living room to talk, yet I'm standing here making declarations and promises that I don't even know if you can quite believe since you don't really know me yet. But you will know me, Melody. I wanted to get to know you before this happened. I feel as if we were on the verge of something more than just friendship and a few text messages before all of this happened, and I know everything's going to change, but I want you to know that you can count on me. And, I guess I have a lot more on my mind than I thought."

And because Fox had said the exact right thing and she didn't have the words herself, she went up onto her toes and kissed him. It was only supposed to be a brush of lips, a sweet embrace to say *thank you* for being the man he was, but as soon as her lips pressed against his, she knew she would be lost in him until the end of days.

They had so much to talk about, so many plans to make and details to hash out. Her life was a roller coaster of endless decisions and responsibilities, but all she wanted to do was push that all out the window and ignore it—just for now. All of the decisions and plans would still be there waiting even if she let go, so she parted her lips and deepened the kiss, knowing that this might be a mistake, but realizing it was a mistake worth making.

She clung to him, and he did the same with her, his hands roaming down her back to cup her butt and press her closer to his hips. She could feel the long line of his erection pressed into her stomach, and she gasped out a breath, forcing herself to try and slow down.

Fox pulled away, as well, his breath coming in hard pants also. "That was… I think it was better than the first time.

And I didn't think that was possible." She licked her lips, and this time, pressed her hands to her belly. Fox caught the motion, and his eyes darkened. He didn't pale, he didn't freak out. He looked…happy.

And yet she had no idea what she was feeling.

"I know we need to talk, but I think I need to go back home for a minute and just breathe. Because I don't want to do something stupid and ruin everything. Because it's not just you and me anymore. And that scares me."

Fox stuffed his hands into his pockets and nodded. "Can I walk you back? I know you walked over here on your own, but it's a nice day out. I promise I won't touch you, I won't even talk if you don't want to. But I just want to be by your side. I know this is crazy, and I know we have a thousand things to talk about, but I think our being in each other's presence is one of those things."

"I think I'd like that. I know I sound like a tease and am throwing a hundred different things at you and then running away. But kissing you like that, when we need to talk and let our minds actually come to terms with our realities, probably wasn't the best way to go about things."

"Just one step at a time. We can do that. Right?"

"I have no idea, but I guess we'd better try." Fox threw on some shoes, and because the two of them apparently liked flirting with danger, they held hands as he walked her back to her grandmother's place. The sun was still shining, and the birds chirped in the air as they turned the corner and headed up the drive to Grandma Pearl's beautiful home. Melody knew she was blessed that she still had family left who wanted her to be a part of their lives, and every time she walked up the stone walkway, she remembered that fact.

But as she looked at the porch and froze, she couldn't help but think that maybe she had made a mistake.

"Someone left flowers?"

She'd almost forgotten that Fox was by her side as she stood there in front of the porch and looked down at the two-dozen roses lying in front of the door. She didn't know why she was so creeped out, but there was something so familiar about those roses. She'd gotten countless similar bouquets back when she was dancing. They'd always just shown up in her dressing room after her performances, and she'd loved the smell of them at the time.

But these had just been casually thrown on the welcome mat, and it didn't make any sense. And she could've sworn she spotted the ribbon to a ballet slipper wrapped around the stems.

She had to be imagining it. Because that just made no sense to her. Then Fox went to pick them up and held out a note.

"It's addressed to you."

"What does it say?" Her voice sounded hollow, even to her own ears. Fox must have heard the note in her voice, too, because he frowned and slowly read what was on the back of the card.

"I know. You can't hide forever." He looked up at her, eyes wide. "What the fuck does that mean?"

She shook her head, her hands shaking, as well. "I...I really don't know." Because she didn't. She couldn't. It had to be a trick or a horrible prank gone wrong. Because she didn't know anyone who would send her those notes and emails.

And yet, here they were, written in echoes and ink, a flash from her past that made her want to curl up into a ball and hide away again.

"I don't know," she whispered again. And this time when Fox held her, she didn't cling back, didn't kiss him. She let him comfort her.

Because she had no idea what was happening, but she had a feeling this was only the beginning.

Chapter 13

Fox sat at his brother's bar, knowing that he needed to get his thoughts in order, but with so many going through his head at once, he had no idea where to start. Melody had told him he could tell his family about the baby since she had a feeling there wouldn't be any hiding it soon given how far along she was, but even then, his mind wasn't on the news he was about to tell.

He was damn worried about those flowers and that note they'd found on the porch. And though she had looked shaken at first, she had shrugged it off, saying that it must be a prank from a kid or something silly. She'd said there was no reason to worry, even though that's all he'd been doing. And though they had a thousand different things on their minds right then, and had more than one life-altering circumstance slamming into them, he wasn't going to let those flowers and that note go. Only the fact that Ms. Pearl's house had a kickass security system installed by his brother had allowed Fox to leave Melody and her grandmother at the house at all.

In fact, he'd be talking to Loch to see if there was anything else they could do about the place.

He frowned, sipping his lime and soda. He knew he might be overreacting, and damn sure overstepping if he was planning to talk to his brother behind the ladies' backs about security, so maybe he should stop and think for a second.

Because finding out that he was going to be a father in a few months had seriously knocked him off his feet, and he wasn't sure what the hell would happen next.

"You're sitting here drinking lime and soda after five?" Loch asked as he took the stool next to Fox. "What's wrong?"

Fox stared at the little lime wedge in his glass and shrugged. "Nothing."

"Well, that was a lie if I've ever heard one," Dare said as he walked up to them on the other side of the bar. "What's wrong?"

"I'm fine." He sipped his drink, doing his best to avoid both of his brothers' eyes. He knew it wouldn't work for long, and he *had* come to the bar to tell them about Melody and the baby, but he still fell out of sorts. Once again, he had no idea what he was doing, and he hated that feeling.

"It's not busy here yet since half the town is at the game, so I can sit here and stare at you until you tell me. I'm good at that." Dare leaned against the bar, his eyes on Fox's.

Loch twisted on his stool so Fox could feel him staring, as well, and he knew that he'd break soon. His brothers had perfected this routine over time, and he knew when to give up.

"You're making this really hard to keep to myself when you keep staring at me like the weirdos you both are."

"Then our job will be complete once you fess up and tell

us what's on your mind." Dare raised his brow, and Fox had a feeling that Loch was doing the same on his other side.

"You know Melody?"

"The woman opening up the new dance studio next to my place? Yeah. We know her. What did you do?"

Fox scowled. "Why do you think I did anything? I'm the one sitting here frustrated."

"Because you are a man, so it has to be your fault. But let's not get off track. Melody. Yes, we know her. I remember her from that first night when you and she were in here pounding down whiskey and thought the rest of us didn't notice."

Fox let out a breath. He hadn't actually known that everyone had been looking at them, but then again, his mind had been on whiskey and Melody. And, honestly, that hadn't really changed.

"If you saw us together, then you probably know that we left together that night."

His brothers didn't say anything, but they both nodded. He could go into every single detail and try to figure out how he was going to tell the people closest to him that he was going to be a father, but for all the words that he knew and used every day in his life and in his passions, he couldn't think of a damn thing to say.

"She's pregnant."

"Say that again." Dare leaned closer, his eyes wide.

"My girl is pregnant." He hadn't actually meant to call Melody his girl, but then again, it felt right to say it. They hadn't talked about what the baby would mean for them, or what it would do to whatever relationship they had, but with this new life they created between them, everything had changed. They would be forever connected, no matter what happened in the future. And that should've probably scared him beyond all reason, but it didn't. In fact, it gave him…he wanted to say purpose but he wasn't even sure that was the right word.

He'd spent so long feeling as though he were falling behind, and that everything was happening at once, that he couldn't quite pull together the right idea of what he should be thinking now. Because the fact that Melody was pregnant really hadn't hit him yet. He could say the words and try to think about the ramifications, but it didn't really feel real. Add that to the fact that every time he was near Melody, he couldn't help but want her, couldn't help but want her in his life, and he knew that he needed to slow the fuck down and get his thoughts in order. Because he was starting to scare himself, and he knew that he would scare Melody away just as easily if she heard the thoughts running through his head at a thousand miles per hour.

"What?" Dare's voice brought Fox out of his thoughts. "Who is pregnant? Melody? She's your girl? When the fuck did all this happen? Did you say pregnant? Oh, God, I think I need to sit down."

"If you can keep your voice down, that would be really helpful. We haven't actually told anyone else, even though she said I could tell the two of you. And we are in a public place, even though no one else is around right now. So, if you could stop screaming that word, that would be really helpful."

"She's your girl?"

Fox turned to Loch, his mouth gaping. "That's what you got out of that? That I called Melody my girl? Because I really think there's something a little bit more important in what I just said that you're sort of glazing over."

"I'm not glazing over anything. I'm trying to figure out

exactly what is going on. Dare is over there looking like he's about to have a stroke, and I'm a little bit behind. So slow it down for us. She's your girl?"

That was possibly the most words his brother had ever said in a full sentence without breathing.

"You know what, screw it, come with me to my office. I really don't want to have to explain to the guests why I'm freaking out and why Fox seems to be staring at his drink—without alcohol by the way—and acting as if nothing is wrong."

Thinking that was probably a good idea, Fox followed Dare and Loch into Dare's office. He couldn't believe that he'd actually just blurted that out like he had, and he had no idea what to say now. But it wasn't as if he could backtrack and pretend that nothing had happened. He couldn't pretend that Melody wasn't pregnant. He couldn't pretend that their one night together didn't have consequences beyond an awkward morning after, and he couldn't pretend that he would be fine doing everything alone while he tried to figure out what the next step was. His family was close for a reason, and he really just needed to talk to his brothers. Then he could find the courage to talk to his sister and his parents. And then maybe he could figure out how to talk to Melody. He'd already been trying to think of ways into her life before everything changed, and now he knew it would be just that much harder. So, yes, he needed to talk to his brothers and get his thoughts in order so he didn't make a mistake and act like a fucking asshole. Because when Fox got stressed and confused, that's exactly what he turned into. And he had no desire to be that kind of man.

Or that kind of father.

Oh, God. *Father*. He kept thinking the word, and now his

stomach hurt. Thankfully, as he sat down in one of the chairs in his brother's office, Dare held out a glass of whiskey, and Fox clung to it as if it would save his life.

"Bottoms up." Dare met his gaze, and Fox figured the panic there was probably only a fraction of what was in his own eyes. Because the more he let the situation sink in, the more he wanted to run around screaming.

Both his brothers held their glasses, and the three of them drowned the shot in one. The burn felt damn good down his throat, the smoky flavor perfection. Of course, it was his brother's whiskey so it would be the best taste for any situation. That was one thing his family did right, and one thing the town was known for. Its whiskey. He never would have figured that he would need it and tradition to calm down after finding out that he had gotten a woman pregnant after a one-night stand. He was truly a fumbling idiot.

"You're going to have to break this down to us step-by-step," Loch said slowly from Fox's other side.

"And make it slow," Dare added.

"I met Melody that night in the bar. I didn't know she was moving here, and I don't think she knew until halfway through our night that I actually lived here. We had too much whiskey, and then we went back to my place. I'm not going to give you the details of that, but needless to say, dear God."

Thankfully, his brothers didn't comment on that, but they did toast him with their empty glasses.

"I figured I would never see her again, even though I kind of wanted to. I don't even know what that means, and now it's even more confusing, but I digress. Three months later, she showed back up in town, and I found out she actually moved here. You know that she's Ms. Pearl's granddaughter and that she's opening up a dance studio. The two of us have slowly been becoming friends because I actually really like her and, yeah, the sex was fucking fantastic, but I also like her as a person. And then, apparently, when Kenzie and Ainsley came to the dance studio, Melody passed out, and they took her to the hospital where she found out she was pregnant. The girls don't actually know that she's pregnant because she wanted to tell me or her grandmother first, but yeah, Melody is pregnant. She's having my baby. And she's over three months along, meaning I have even less time than usual to figure out what the hell to do. What the hell *we're* going to do. In other words, I'm freaking out, and I think I need another glass of whiskey."

Dare poured another glass for the three of them without a word. He knew Loch needed to work later that night, and Dare was on shift, and neither of them usually drank when they worked. But finding out that one of their own was going to be a dad was a good reason for booze. They took the shots like the first, the burn a little smoother this time. Then Fox set down his glass and shook his head when Dare held up the rest of the bottle.

"Whiskey is what got me into this situation in the first place. I think two is more than enough."

"Good point." Dare put away the bottle then folded his arms over his chest, mirroring Loch's position. Fox sat on the chair, his elbows on his knees, and his head in his hands.

"I have no idea what I'm doing."

"But you're doing it," Loch said softly. "You're going to be a father. I'm not going to ask if you actually think the baby is yours because you're not one to trust easily. You've seen the hell that Dare and I went through when it came to our kids, and I know you'll try to do a better job than we did."

"Not going to be hard, since I pretty much sucked at

trying to get custody because of my job and my injury." Dare shook his head but didn't continue. Fox didn't blame him since it had taken a while for his brother to get over everything that had happened.

"I trust her. And if it comes to needing actual results or tests or anything like that, I'm sure we can figure it out, but you didn't see her, you guys. She looked just as pale and scared as I do. She came here to start a new life and to open up her studio, and she ended up pregnant because she and I couldn't keep our hands off each other. I've no idea what I'm going to do, and I have no idea what the two of us are going to do. But in the end, we're going to have to do something. Because she's pregnant. And those months will go by fast."

"Well, you're not alone." At Loch's words, Fox nodded. There wasn't really anything else to say because there was such promise behind those words, they meant everything.

"And I take it you've known about this for probably less than a day. You don't need to have all the answers now. And I'm sure there will be more questions before you can even figure out the first answer, but like Loch said, you're not alone. And you know Mom and Dad are going to be over the moon at the thought of having another grandchild. Plus, with Tabby pregnant, it's gonna make for cousins, so they'll be beyond excited…even if it's scary. But, Fox, you're going to be a dad. That's really fucking awesome."

Fox smiled but leaned back and grinned with his brothers. Because, yeah, things would get even more complicated soon, but the fact that he was going to be a dad…that was pretty damn amazing.

Chapter 14

Melody needed to just bite the bullet and get this over with. Because the more she hid within herself, the worse it would be when the time came. Or at least that's what she had learned after so many years of not being the best person. She hated lying and keeping secrets, and that meant she needed to tell her grandmother about the baby. Because it changed everything.

She'd come to town because her grandmother had said she needed her, even though Melody still wasn't 100% sure that was the case. She'd also come to town to open up her own studio, and all of that might be derailed because of the baby growing inside of her.

She placed her hand on her stomach and let out a deep breath. *It isn't the baby's fault*, she thought. But the timing sucked.

Fox was telling his brothers tonight about the pregnancy, and now it was her turn to tell her grandmother. She had a feeling her grandma already knew something was off, but Melody figured there was no way she could guess *this*.

She did her best to shake off her nervousness and left her room to make her way through the house to where her grandmother sat by a small fire, reading a book.

Grandma Pearl had once been a showgirl, but she had been the classiest one in Melody's mind. Now, her grandmother looked as if she belonged in Regency England, reading or cross-stitching and waiting for tea after ringing the bell for the butler. If that was how that all worked. The only real Regency era information she knew came from romances, and she usually paid more attention to the dukes than the tea.

"If you don't come in and tell me what's on your mind, I'm going to have to start making guesses myself, and we both know that could end up terribly. For all I know, you're going to leave me to go join the circus and get tattooed from head to toe. Not that there's anything wrong with that, but I might talk you out of it so you can stay in Whiskey."

Melody grinned despite herself and took a seat across from her grandmother. "Have I said thank you recently? Thank you for taking me in. Thank you for offering to take me in many times before this even though I didn't deserve it. Thank you for always sending flowers and coming to all of my recitals and performances at Juilliard. Thank you for believing in me when I said I was ready to open up a studio in a small town that I wasn't part of. Thank you for making this place a home for me. Have I said all of that recently?"

Her grandmother smiled softly, a single tear tracing down her cheek. Melody hated to see it, so she got up quickly and used a tissue from the side table to wipe her grandmother's face.

"Don't cry." *Please don't cry, because you might start crying again soon when I tell you that I'm pregnant and unwed.* Not that her grandmother was very traditional, but one never knew in this type of situation.

"I'm going to cry if I want to. Because, yes, you said thank you recently. You always find ways to say thank you even if it's not words. But your words just now were beautiful, and I love you so much, Melody. I'm so glad that you're finally here. It's like my home has been waiting for you. You fit right in. Now why don't you tell me what's on your mind, because I know it wasn't just to say thank you? Something's wrong, baby. You can tell me. I promise I'll be here for you no matter what."

This time, it was Melody who let a few tears fall, but she didn't bother wiping them away. She had a feeling there would be more soon.

"I don't know how to tell you this, so I'm just going to say the words." She took a deep breath. "I'm pregnant."

Her grandmother blinked for a few moments before nodding. "Now your nausea and your little hospital visit that you did not tell me about make sense. Are you okay? Are you feeling okay?"

Melody sat there for a second, trying to figure out exactly what had just happened. "How on earth did you find out that I went to the hospital? Isn't there some patient confidentiality thing?"

Her grandmother rolled her eyes as if she were Melody's age or younger. The movement was just so much like her own that Melody couldn't help the small smile that played on her face, even though her nerves were worse than ever.

"Your doctor didn't tell me, if that is what you're worried about. A friend was there picking up a prescription and happened to see you. Remember, granddaughter of mine, I have ears and eyes everywhere. I see and know all. That is the mysteriousness of Ms. Pearl."

She waved her arms around her face as if she were a fifties starlet, and it sent them both into a fit of soft laughter. Then her grandmother stood up and went to sit by Melody on the loveseat.

"You're pregnant. Going to have a baby. I am going to be a great-grandmother. Possibly the most gorgeous great-grandmother out there, but that is neither here nor there. Really, how are you feeling?"

"Like I'm going to throw up, but I don't know if that's because of the morning sickness since it doesn't actually happen only in the mornings, or the fact that everything is happening all at once. I'm really overwhelmed."

"Well, that makes sense. It wouldn't be a pregnancy if you didn't feel like you had to throw up every five minutes. And since you just found out, I assume that it hasn't really hit yet, and you have more questions than answers, and even more questions that you don't even know you should be asking yet. What does Fox have to say about it?"

Melody froze. "Fox?"

"Yes, Fox." Her grandmother patted her hand. "You know, the father of your child. There's only one man in this town that I've seen you go doe-eyed over. And I do not need to know all the details, though you can tell me. I have probably seen and done more than you could ever dream of, but that is for the next editorial." She winked, and Melody laughed again. "But, yes, Fox. I saw the way you two looked at each other. And that look had nothing to do with first meetings and simple crushes. And the timing does make sense. So, what does Fox have to say?"

Grandma Pearl really did see all and know all. Melody

should have known she wouldn't be able to hide her feelings, whatever they were, for Fox from her grandmother for long. But it turned out she hadn't hidden them at all.

"He's supportive. I really don't know more, other than the fact that he rambled like I did and said he's going to be here for the baby and me no matter what. We haven't actually had a chance to talk about all the details of what that means because I don't know the details or anything. I never thought I'd be a mom. Not that I thought I wouldn't be a mom. It was more like my life was just about dancing, and then when that changed, having a family didn't really factor into the picture. And having a baby with a man that I only know somewhat and I've only been with once? I feel like I'm two steps behind and can't catch up."

Her grandmother wrapped her arm around Melody's shoulders and held her close. "When I found out that I was pregnant with your mother, I thought my world had shattered. Yet it bloomed all at the same time. She was a surprise, but never a mistake. And I feel like maybe you feel the same way. So take a couple of days to let yourself roll in the chaos and then be the woman that I know you are and conquer everything. You're going to make mistakes, I sure as hell did. But I know you're going to be a wonderful mother because you've been through hell and back, and you know what it means to make the wrong choices. You're going to make sure your children never have to make the choices you did. Those babies will never feel like they aren't enough. So take time to breathe, then do what you need to do to become prepared, and then figure out what you want with the father of your child—the man who looks at you like he wants to eat you up. Because, baby, I did not miss that look, and I have a feeling you did not miss it either."

Oddly relieved, Melody talked with her grandmother for a few moments more, and then it was time for Grandma Pearl to start her nightly routine and head to bed. It was still early yet, but her grandmother liked to read in bed with a facemask or two. Melody was trying to learn the same routine because she wanted skin like that when she was her grandmother's age.

The doorbell rang, the gong startling her as always right as her grandmother walked upstairs. Melody waved her off so she wouldn't have to come back down. She didn't know who would be at the house at that time of night, but it might be Fox. The two of them did need to talk, and if he was as scattered as she was, it would make sense that he would show up without warning. But when she opened the door, it wasn't Fox.

"Kenzie. Ainsley. Hi."

Kenzie winced, and Ainsley waved. "Sorry we're here unannounced."

"But Fox told us the news. I don't know if he was supposed to, but we sort of walked in on the guys talking and being secretive, and we're really good at ferreting information. So, sorry we made him spill the beans, but we're here for you." Ainsley beamed, looking far too gorgeous for her own good.

"Oh." Melody's mouth went dry. "You know."

Kenzie nodded then opened her arms. "Yep. And we're here for girl time, so hug me, and then we can talk, eat junk food, or sit and watch movies."

And because this town had once again opened its heart for her in the form of these two women, Melody went straight into Kenzie's arms and held the other woman tightly. Ainsley hugged her from behind, and the three of them stood on her porch, not saying a word, yet saying plenty.

Melody might not know what she was going to do about being a mother, and she had no idea what to do about her relationship with Fox, but the strong women surrounding her and the strongest woman she knew being upstairs in the house, meant that she wasn't alone.

And that might not mean much to someone else, but for a person who hadn't had a single friend—not really—because she was too focused on dancing competitions, it meant the world to Melody.

And when the three broke apart, she let her new friends into the house and listened as they talked about nothing at all. And they didn't actually talk about why they had come in the first place. Somehow, they just knew she needed to breathe. Somehow.

Her phone buzzed.

Fox: *The girls are on their way over or already there. Didn't want you to be alone, and figured you needed time away from me to think.*

Not so mysterious after all, Melody thought. The man knew her more than she thought possible, and they'd only been texting and in each other's lives for a short while. She knew that could be dangerous, but she also knew she would risk it anyway. At least for now.

Melody: *Thank you. They're taking care of me.*

Fox: *Good. They're great women. Two of the best in my life. Glad you aren't alone. See you tomorrow?*

The girls were staring at her as she texted, and she knew she'd tell them afterward, but she ignored them for now, her attention on her phone and Fox. Did she want to see him tomorrow? Of course, she did. And not just because their lives would be forever intertwined. She'd wanted to know more about him before, even if she wouldn't have had that kind of time with how things were, and now things had changed. And she really wanted to know Fox. Wanted to know the man that was the father of her child. Wanted to know the man himself.

So she texted him that she would see him tomorrow, knowing that they might be taking a step into something that could possibly hurt them both, or at least change everything. She didn't have the answers. As it turned out, she didn't have the answer to many things. Seeing as she had spent most of her life focused on something that had turned out to be wrong for her soul, maybe it was time to figure out who this new person in the mirror was, and see how Fox and their new future could fit together.

Chapter 15

Fox probably shouldn't have been nervous to show Melody around town, considering they had already slept together and had spent time together, but he was still nervous as hell. After he had told his brothers the news, Kenzie and Ainsley had shown up soon after, demanding to know what had the three Collins brothers so on edge. And because Dare didn't want to hide things from his woman, and Loch had a strange relationship with his best friend, Fox didn't bother keeping secrets.

The two of them had looked shocked for a moment and then had squealed before hugging him. Then they had left the three guys alone because they wanted to talk to Melody. Sure, it had been his idea because he didn't want Melody to be alone while family surrounded him, but the girls had made it sound as if it was their idea, as well. He didn't mind because while Melody had her grandmother, Fox had so many more people in his life. And that meant there were many more shoulders he could lean on. And while he wanted to be a shoulder Melody could lean on, he had a feeling that they'd both needed space the night before. At least she might have needed space from him. He could be wrong, but by sending the girls over there, at least he'd known she wasn't alone.

And now, Melody was on her way over to his office so they could take a late lunch/early dinner together and so he could show her around town. She'd been living in Whiskey for a little bit now and had visited before, but she had said that she didn't know some of the little histories that came with each block and building. She might know the tourist's version of the bootlegging stories, but there was so much more to Whiskey than its namesake.

The grand opening of her dance studio was soon, and he knew she was beyond nervous and frazzled. He had offered to help, and other than putting a notice in his paper that she had paid for, that was all she had allowed him to do until the day of. She planned to have a party to celebrate all of the new students and the building itself. And figured that would be a great time for everyone to get to know her as well as for her to check out who would be entering her classrooms. Fox would be there to be her errand boy, and he didn't mind. Loch had also offered, even though he was also going as the father of one of the students. Fox had a feeling his entire family would show up and make sure Melody wasn't alone for even a moment. She had no idea what she had signed on for when she slept with him, but neither had he. He hadn't known he would find the most interesting, intelligent, sexy woman he could've ever hoped for. And he was glad that they would have this afternoon to get to know each other.

And that meant he needed to make sure that she enjoyed herself. Because if he made the town sound like a dull place today, she might think that he was dull and never want to see him again. Hell, he sounded as if he were back in high school again, worried about what the girls thought about him and his skinny limbs. He might've filled out in the muscle department, but apparently, the nerves department hadn't changed much.

Melody had said that she would meet him in front of the office so she wouldn't bother him at work, and since it was time, Fox packed up his things and headed out past his writers' desks. Nancy looked up, narrowed her eyes, then went back to work. He barely resisted rolling his eyes at her. They would have to figure out a way to work together, especially if she continued to act as if she could write anything she wanted and however long she wanted it. Sometimes, he really hated the whole being a boss thing.

He had a feeling Nancy wouldn't be staying at the paper much longer. He didn't plan to fire her because she did damn good work. But he figured she wouldn't stay because the small town just wasn't enough for her. She'd end up moving to a bigger paper with bigger news eventually, and that was just fine with him. Whiskey wasn't for everyone—the town or the drink.

Melody was standing on the sidewalk right outside his building when he walked out. She wore leggings, ballet flats, and this tunic thing that cinched in at her waist and showcased her figure. He'd always known she was sexy. Had felt her sweet curves beneath his hands, but right then, he couldn't help but think she was even sexier. And, yeah, he couldn't stop his gaze from darting to her stomach, nor could he ignore the warmth filling him. Yeah, he was nervous and scared, but he was also damn excited. They were going to have a baby. He loved kids. And at this point in his life, he'd thought he would've had kids of his own by now. The fact that Melody was going to have his child made him feel like a Neanderthal, wanting to pound his chest and say that, yes, he had done that. And that was why he was never, ever going to tell Melody that train of thought.

"Hey there. I'm glad you came."

Melody turned at the sound of his voice, her eyes brightening. He was glad they did that rather than having her shrink away in fear or whatever. He was seriously nervous about this day, and he just hoped that he didn't screw it all up.

"I'm glad I came, too. I want to know more about the town since I'm planning to stay here for a good while. And I could use a walk. I've been inside that studio for so long now, that I think I've paced every single step. It's pretty much done, and I'm so nervous for tomorrow." She rested her hand on her stomach, and his gaze couldn't pull away. He wanted to put his hand over hers, but he had a feeling that neither of them was ready for that. Or maybe they were and he was just scared.

"I've seen the place, remember? It looks great, and you're going to do great."

"You say that, but now that I'm pregnant, it changes things."

He held back a wince, knowing that being a dance instructor while pregnant probably wasn't the easiest thing to do. But then again, he didn't actually know the ins and outs of her days—that was something he wanted to change.

"We'll figure it out. Just remember, you're not alone in this. We're the ones having this baby. So we're the ones who will make the plans. But first, let me show you Whiskey. Maybe when you get to know the town, and tomorrow when the town gets to know you even more, you can feel a little more settled. Because, yeah, I'm just as nervous as you are about what's going to happen in the next few months, but I think knowing what's around you and maybe having that touchstone will help. Or I'm just blowing smoke up your ass and trying to think of a way for us to go on a date in the middle the day since we both have other things to do."

That made Melody laugh, and he was glad for it. "It's not really the middle the day. You only took the last hour off work, and at this point, I think it'll probably count as lunch. I'm sorry we had to push it back a couple hours, but I was in the groove at the studio and didn't want to break it. You know?"

"Actually, I don't. I don't really groove."

"You grooved that night. And…I can't believe I actually just said that out loud. It's not like we're really going to ignore what happened, and we're both trying to figure out if we want to work together as a couple or friends or co-parents or whatever and I'm freaking myself out. But yeah, you had moves, good moves."

If Fox were a peacock, he would have preened and spread his feathers at that point. Why that image popped into his head, he didn't know.

"You had pretty good moves yourself, Melody. Just saying." And because he remembered the moves, his cock pressed into the zipper of his jeans, and he had to clear his throat. Her gaze traveled down his body and landed on where his visible erection strained against the denim. There was no hiding it, and even though he should have been embarrassed, he wasn't. Because Melody was the one who had done that to him. He could see the sharp pebbles of her nipples pressing against her shirt, and he knew that he wasn't the only one turned on.

He swallowed hard, and then held out his hand, determined not to act the fool and kiss her right there on the sidewalk where anyone could see. He'd promised her a view of the town, and that's what she'd get.

And he'd do his best to learn to walk with a hard-on from hell.

As he'd been in this situation a few times now thanks to Melody, he learned quickly.

"Ready to see Whiskey?" He hoped his voice sounded calm and not like he wanted to jump her. When she took a deep breath and took his hand, he had a feeling the walk would end up a different form of torture for both of them.

"Sounds good to me. Are there ghost stories? I love ghost stories."

"There's a few," he said as they made their way down the street so they were on Main. "Though I think the most famous one is where they thought Ms. Pearl was the lady in white in the attic."

Melody's eyes widened, and she laughed, the sound filling him, drawing him near. "That sounds like her. She probably put on the getup just to get a rise out of people."

"And since I might have reminded her of the story when we were talking, she said she might do it again." He gave her a pained grimace, but she laughed.

"She'll probably rope me into it, and I'll be in another window in the attic dressed all in white so I can scare the children, too."

"You know, she'd probably put you in the outfit from Swan Lake so you could dance in the widow instead." They made a turn so he could show her the bridge where they would easily walk from Pennsylvania to New Jersey, ending up in both places at once at a certain point, something that tourists loved to do.

"Oh, God. She totally would. I'd have to be on pointe too because Grandma doesn't do things halfway."

"Don't put ideas into her head because you know she'll do it." He squeezed her hand, and she smiled up at him. "Okay, so this is the main bridge that gets us from Whiskey to the New Jersey side of the Delaware. This is the newer bridge. The original one from back when the town was founded had to be taken down due to safety issues, but it's still pretty damn old. And in a few feet, you'll be able to stand in both states at once, something you'll need a photo of at least once if you want to be a Whiskey resident."

"Is it wrong that I'm oddly excited about that fact? I saw it in a movie once and thought it was the most romantic gift ever because the heroine was sick, and the hero wanted her to have all her wishes."

Fox squeezed her hand again and tugged her close so someone could walk on the other side of them. Only one side of the bridge was for pedestrian traffic so they couldn't take up too much room. He let go of her hand as she sank into his side and he wrapped his arm around her shoulders, tightening his hold.

He liked the feeling of her against him, the idea that the woman carrying his child was touching him. He might be a caveman thinking that, but he didn't care. He wanted more of this, wanted more of Melody. How much she gave of herself, however, wasn't something he could find out just by holding her close. It would take time, and no matter how close he felt to her, how much he felt as if he knew her, they were still almost strangers. Strangers who were having a baby and slowly going down a path of a potential relationship. His head started to spin at how quickly everything had changed, but he had to remind himself that no matter how complicated things got, he had to live in the moment, as well.

"Fox? Are you okay? We're at the line."

He blinked, pushing away the thoughts that could get him into trouble, and kissed the top of her head before looking down at the line that demarcated the division between the two states. They were standing over the Delaware River, people milling about, and yet his whole world was in his arms right then.

If that didn't send a shock through him, he didn't know what would.

"Let's get you your photo."

"Want me to take a picture of you both?" a woman said from beside them. "I always hate when all my photos of this spot end up with just my feet and not my face."

Fox smiled and nodded. "That'd be great. Thanks." He looked down at Melody. "Ready to play tourist?"

"Always." He handed over his phone, and Melody turned in his arms so he leaned against the railing and she was in front of him, his arms wrapped around her. Without conscious thought, he splayed his hand over her belly, and she froze for a moment before realizing, her hand tangling with his so they could both cradle their child.

Holy shit.

Their baby. As in a new life forming under his hand at that very moment. As the woman took their photo, he knew this point in time would be forever immortalized. And he knew when he saw photo or the line again, he'd always remember the fact that he'd been reeling inside even as he held Melody for what felt like the first and hundredth time.

How it could feel so right so quickly, he didn't know, but he knew he didn't want to let her go. He kissed the top of her head again, trying to tone down the emotions and perhaps even the possessiveness that warred through him.

She shook against him, and he had a feeling something was going through her system just as it was for him. He thanked the woman and took back his phone, and without words, he and Melody made their way to the other side of the bridge, then turned back so they could walk through Whiskey. Just as he was about to stop by the bar for lunch, knowing that while there were plenty of other places to eat, his family bar was a favorite and something that would always be a part of his—and now perhaps her—life, Melody put her hand on his arm and stopped him.

"What's wrong? Would you rather go somewhere you haven't been before to eat? That probably would have made more sense, but the girls will be at the bar tonight, as will my brothers, so I figured you might want to hang with people you know. But now that I say that, it doesn't sound like a date. It feels a bit overwhelming. I can easily take you to another place. Sorry I didn't even ask you, I was just playing tourist."

She smiled, her head shaking as he continued to talk.

"What?"

"You just rounded yourself into like four issues I don't even have with what you planned. I've *loved* today, and though it should have felt weird and awkward since it's technically our first date, it wasn't. I'm having a wonderful time, but I'm also a little tired." She held up her hand when he would have rambled more. "I'm fine. How about we get something from the bar and take it to your house?" She swallowed hard. "I, uh…I'd like some time alone with you, too. I know we're doing a great job of not talking about what's growing inside me right now since I know we're both still shocked, but what I *do* know is that we need to get to know each other. And I'd like to try and do that tonight."

There was an underlying heat in her words that made him want to bring her close and crush his mouth to hers. And because he knew that wouldn't be the best idea when they were both standing outside his brother's bar, he kissed her temple instead and pulled back, loving the way her eyes darkened at the touch of his lips on her skin. Oh, yeah, he wasn't alone in this need, and yet they were both being so damn careful about not doing anything about it.

Yet.

Thankfully, when he went inside with Melody, he quickly got a takeout order from one of Dare's waitresses and somehow avoided his family and the other ladies. While he wanted them to see him with Melody, he also wanted to be alone with her.

Before he knew it, the two of them were in his house, under the same roof where he'd had her in his arms before, and all he could do was stare at her like a man beyond thirsty for the oasis in front of him.

The thing was, though, he could tell he wasn't alone in this hunger. Melody stared at him, her mouth parted, her eyes wide, her breaths coming in pants. There was a sexual energy between them that sizzled, crackling as it danced along their skin.

"The food's going to get cold if you keep looking at me like that," he growled. He hadn't meant to growl, to even say that, but they hadn't even taken off their shoes yet, and all he could do was *need*.

"You know we should talk," she said, though he wasn't sure she believed her words.

"We did. We talked about Whiskey. Talked about my family. Talked about Ms. Pearl. Your dance studio." They hadn't talked about the baby, her dancing, her parents, his writing, but those things would come.

First, however…

She stepped forward, the first to close the distance, and it nearly sent him over the edge. Then she put her fingertips on his chest, and he nearly shook.

"I know we should, but I don't want to talk. Not right now. We have time. Right now, I want to do something that might be a mistake, and might make me go running again, but I don't care. I should. But I don't."

He cupped her face, her cheeks in his palms soft. "We will. But for now, tell me you want this. Tell me you want me."

She snorted. "Of course, I want you, Fox. I've wanted you from the first moment I saw you, and it wasn't because of the whiskey. As for this? Yes. But no promises. I can't…I can't make those kinds of promises. Though we should since this isn't just about the two of us, but I can't."

He nodded, not hurt in the slightest since her words mirrored his thoughts. "I can do that. Because we're not done, you and me. That's the only promise I can make."

And in answer, she went on her tiptoes, so he leaned down, meeting her halfway to take her lips with his own.

She closed the distance so she was pressed firmly against him. Their mouths pressed harder, the kiss deepening. His hands slid from her cheeks down her body so he could grip her hips. Her arms wrapped around his middle, his erection a firm line against her belly. He was so hard from the mere kiss that he knew if he weren't careful, he'd blow right there and make a fool of himself.

But with Melody, he didn't know if he'd mind acting the fool. Because with her, he could be his ramble-filled self who didn't make much sense, and growl and stare off into the distance as he thought too hard.

She pinched his side and winked. "Mr. Writer is thinking too hard again. Just kiss me. And maybe get me naked. How about we go upstairs to that bed I know because, while I'm flexible, I'm really not in the mood to get stair marks on my ass."

He laughed, taking her lips with his before bending down so he could hold her in his arms. She let out a gasp as she wrapped her hands over his shoulders.

"Fox!"

"Well, since you're in a delicate condition, I figured I shouldn't let you walk up stairs." He was careful as he practically ran up the stairs, eager to have her in his bed again.

"I'm about to run a dance studio, I think I can handle stairs." He set her down in front of the bed, careful not to jostle her. She was his and, hell, she was carrying their child. Shit, he needed to stop thinking that or he'd freak out. He promised himself that he'd handle it all soon. But for now, he wanted Melody naked.

"Fine, how about I just wanted you up here quickly so I could lick between your legs?"

She smiled, didn't blush at all before giving him a nod. "You know what? I can handle that. Now get stripping."

He laughed. Fucking *laughed* as he stripped off his shirt and helped her take off her clothes, as well. Somehow, the two of them ended up tangled in jeans and shoes but still wrapped around each other on the bed, his hands roaming over her curves as he tried to calm himself down. They were both naked, touching everything they could without taking the next step, but they couldn't keep their hands off each other. He remembered their first night together and knew they hadn't taken it this slowly, and for that he was grateful. Now, he could go slower, savor.

That was if Melody's roaming hands on his dick let him.

"Jesus." He closed his eyes, sucking in a breath.

"Just wondering when the licking is going to begin," she said huskily.

"I need to get condoms first because I think my mind is going to be a little too on you and not on being safe."

"You can't get me pregnant again, Fox," she said, her voice soft.

"I know, and I'm clean, but I want you to be safe."

She nodded, letting him get up off the bed so he could grab a condom from the nightstand.

"When we do this again," he continued, "we can get our tests done to make sure we can go condom free."

"When, not if? You're so sure of yourself?" she asked, her head going back as he kissed down her belly and then along each thigh. She let out a moan, and he nipped at her skin, spreading her with his hands so he could get closer to her pussy.

"You're in my skin, Melody, in my bed. I'm not sure of much these days, but I'm sure of the fact that there's something here." And before she could answer, he had his mouth on her, and she was groaning under him. She tasted sweet and *his* and if he weren't careful, he'd fall right then and there. He let his hands roam up to her breasts, pressing his face closer to her pussy. She bent for him, letting him cup her, playing with her nipples. Then he went back to putting his hands on her thighs as she cupped her breasts in her hands.

It was so fucking hot, he almost came again.

But he held back and sucked on her clit, and when she came on his face, he growled into her, the vibration thankfully sending her over the edge again. He quickly sat up, licking her wetness from his lips as he sheathed himself in the condom. Then he was over her, his cock nudging at her entrance. She arched up for him, and he pushed, impaling her in one quick thrust.

They both moaned, but he didn't stop, couldn't. She met him thrust for thrust, their bodies coated in sweat as he turned them over so she could ride him.

She gave him a wink, and he gripped her hips even harder, pounding into her from below even as she rocked her hips. She looked like a blond goddess above him, her rounded curves sexy and alluring, her smoky eyes filled with sex, heat, and need.

And he wanted to provide everything she needed.

So when he flicked his thumb over her clit, and she came, he followed soon after, filling the condom until he knew he'd be spent for hours. She fell on top of him, and he held her close, her breasts pressed into his chest, and his cock still inside her.

They didn't say anything, and when they ate their meal naked in his bedroom and went for round two, they still didn't talk about the important things. And when he walked her home, they *still* didn't. He knew they would, they both talked far too much not to, but he had a feeling that what had happened just now had changed something between them.

What that meant, he didn't know, but he knew they would deal with it. Because he didn't want to let her go. He'd started to fall for Melody, and with each new aspect of her that he discovered, he knew that had always been an inevitability.

Chapter 16

Melody's nerves were causing little sparks to dance over her skin, and she was sure if she stopped moving, she'd fall right then and there. And having the dance instructor fall on the dance floor during the opening day of a dance studio wouldn't make for great business.

She'd spent months getting ready for this day, hours upon hours organizing, setting up loans, designing, and preparing herself to become a teacher in something she'd once thought was more important than breathing. And though she'd found more important things in her life than dancing and had done her best to change her mean-girl attitude since she'd hated the woman she was back then, dance would be at the center of her life once again.

Only, now, there was something far more important than dance, her studio, or anything else she'd ever done, and she was beyond scared and nervous about it. She had no idea what she was going to do when she made it to her third trimester and needed to teach dance, or what would happen when she had to take time off to recuperate after having the baby, or even what she would do once she was ready to teach again but had an infant in her arms.

Melody sucked in a few breaths, trying not to hyperventilate since people would be in her studio at any moment for lemonade, snacks, and conversation.

And the entire time, she was going to do her best to not throw up.

Should be easy enough.

Her stomach rolled.

Or not.

Her grandmother had hired the caterer for the event as a present, though Melody had tried to turn her down. The duo who owned a shop near Dare's bar had already set everything up and departed, and would be back soon to help out with serving and drinks. Soon, Grandma Pearl would be in the studio, and Melody would be able to hug her grandmother and tell her thanks in person. She was always so much steadier when the last of her family was near.

Melody put her hand on her belly and swallowed hard. Not the last, at least not anymore. But she couldn't think about that now. Sure, she'd stayed up reading about what comes next and what expecting a baby meant, but it still hadn't hit her that somehow she'd ended up knocked up on the verge of her new life.

She rolled her shoulders back.

Get a grip, Melody.

It wasn't as if she hadn't had to deal with obstacles before for hell's sake. She'd danced her heart out, put blood, sweat, and tears into her career and what she'd thought would be the only part worth living in her life to become one of the best dancers in the country, and she hadn't even made it to a full company at the time. She'd come back from injury to walk again after finding out her dancing career was over. She'd found herself again after she ran from who she once was. And as each step had tripped her up and forced her into a new stage of her life, she'd come back fighting—even if she hadn't been the same person she was before.

She'd just make a plan. Make lists.

And maybe, just maybe, rely on the man she'd spent the night with. Though that thought might not be something she could quite see through to the end yet, she knew she couldn't run again. She'd moved to Whiskey to put down roots, and it seemed the town had wrapped its own around her in the most unexpected way.

Someone tapped on the door, and she turned on her heel, almost falling in her haste. Once again, she took a deep breath and promised herself that she would *not* fall in front of her new dancers and their families. There was only so much she could take, after all.

Her stomach did that weird fluttering thing that had nothing at all to do with the baby and everything to do with the man at the door. Fox stood there, a grin on his face, and her grandmother by his side. She hadn't known that he planned to bring her grandmother with him. Though her grandma had been very interested in what Fox meant to Melody, she'd been oddly careful about how she answered Grandma Pearl about him. Melody still couldn't quite believe how supportive the other woman had been ever since she told her about the baby, but Melody knew she shouldn't have been surprised.

Her grandmother was *the* Ms. Pearl, after all. She'd insert herself into Melody's life and always be there. No matter what.

Melody quickly made her way to the door to let them in before Fox could knock again. "You're here," she said, her smile widening. She was beyond nervous, perhaps even more so now than she had been while dancing, but seeing the one person who meant the most to her and the other who was quickly sharing that space in her soul calmed her more than she thought possible.

"Of course, we're here," Ms. Pearl said with a wink. "It's our girl's big day. Now give me a hug and let me inside so I can fawn like I'm prone to do when it comes to my baby girl's dreams."

And Melody knew she couldn't hold back anymore. Tears fell down her cheeks, and her grandmother tut-tutted good-naturedly even as Fox wiped the streaks from her face. Grandma Pearl didn't say a word as she strode into the studio, but the man beside her hugged Melody close.

"So damn proud of you," he whispered. "You're kicking ass and taking names, and soon, this place is going to be filled with the people who trust you and want to learn from you. You're amazing."

"And you haven't even seen me dance yet." Something she knew needed to be rectified soon. When, she didn't know, but if this man were going to somehow be part of her life, she had to show him all parts of her.

And tell him who she was.

And what she'd done.

That fast, she was no longer feeling the heat between them, only the coldness that had spread within her through years of mistakes and wrong choices.

Fox seemed to see the change in her, but he didn't

comment. There wasn't any time, and she was so confused and worried that she was making more mistakes. When they were alone, before they could find out who they could be together, she would have to tell him the truth. Because there was no other choice, not anymore.

This wasn't a one-night stand or even a two-night stand. Even if she weren't pregnant, there was still a connection between them that drew her to him, one that seemed to make him do the same with her, and because of that, he needed to know who she truly was.

Who she had been before.

Before Fox could say anything or even pull her away as she thought he might do, the caterers arrived again, and Fox's parents were right behind them. Melody swallowed hard, trying not to freak out because they *knew* about the baby. Once he'd told his brothers, he'd had to tell the elder Collins couple, as well. Fox had warned her that they would probably come since she'd been so busy with work—same as Fox for that matter—but he hadn't had a chance to introduce them like he had with the rest of his family.

And Melody had never felt as if she'd been found lacking as she did right then.

Fox squeezed her hand and led her to the older couple who looked like the parts of Fox she'd seen in the various pieces of his personality.

"Mom, Dad, this is Melody. Melody, these are my parents, Barbara and Bob." Fox wrapped his arm around her waist and kissed the top of her head. Clearly laying claim.

She wasn't going to vomit, but it would be close. She honestly had no idea how her supposedly simplified life had gotten so confusing and complex, but now it seemed as if she didn't have a choice but to face whatever came next.

"We're so happy to finally meet you," Fox's mom said. She reached out and pulled Melody away from Fox and into a tight hug. "We're excited for other reasons, but we can talk about that later," the other woman whispered so only Melody could hear.

For some reason, though she probably should have stiffened at the reminder that Fox's mom knew he'd gotten some random woman pregnant, another kind of warmth filled her instead. Fox's mom seemed…*excited* about what was to come. Or at least she acted that way now and wasn't making a huge deal about it in public since Melody didn't want the news out.

Yes, she should probably tell her new dance students about the baby, but Melody was going to do everything in her power not to interrupt lessons or make her pregnancy interfere with the new studio in any way. She'd find a way to make it work, darn it. And she'd tell them soon, once she actually believed what was going on with her.

"Oh," she finally said, pulling away. *Oh.* Not the most brilliant thing to say, but Fox's mom had left her speechless.

Before she could say anything else, Fox's father was hugging her tight, and then the rest of the Collins family was right behind them. Dare held Kenzie's hand, his son Nate between them as they introduced Melody to her new charge. Loch showed up soon after with his daughter, Misty, in tow and Ainsley right beside them. The three looked so much like a family that it was hard to comprehend that the other woman was just Loch's friend. Again, Melody figured there was a story there, but she didn't say anything. She had enough on her plate as it was.

Soon, the building was bursting with incoming students, their families, townsfolk who wanted to see what the new girl was all about, and her and Fox's family. If she'd had time to be nervous, she might have started shaking, but as it was, the two hours passed by in a blink. She'd spent the entire party going from group to group, introducing herself to everyone she could find and sizing up who would be in her classes. There were so many smiling faces that the excitement started to push away the fear. She knew that if she focused, she could do this.

Even if she were pregnant with a not-so-much-a-stranger-anymore's baby.

Before she knew it, the place had emptied, and Fox's parents had invited her to a family dinner that didn't seem like something she could get out of, and soon, she was standing next to Fox and her grandmother.

Grandma Pearl hugged her close and kissed her cheek. "I'm so proud of you. This place looks wonderful, and the joy in those children's eyes means that you're going to set that spark for them. Even if it's just for a season where they stretch their legs and find out that dancing isn't for them, they're going to have those memories. You're doing something wonderful for this town, and I've never been prouder of you. I can't wait until your little baby grows up to watch you dance and sees how far you've come. You're my inspiration, baby girl. I love you so much."

Melody couldn't help the sting behind her eyes, but she didn't let the tears fall this time. She'd cried enough recently, and honestly, she'd had too good and memorable of a day so far to let tears spoil it—even if they were happy ones.

"Thank you," she whispered, resting her forehead on her grandmother's. "You mean the world to me." Melody missed her parents and knew that though they'd had their faults, they had always believed in her. But right then, it was her grandmother who lifted her up. And unlike before, she never wanted to take that for granted.

"Same here, girl." She kissed Melody's forehead and stood back. "Now, one of my bridge club ladies is outside waiting to take me home so we can have some tea and gossip about who we saw today as that's part of our routine, but you should go see to that young man behind you who's casually leaning against the wall as if he hasn't been watching you with dreamy and intense eyes for the past two hours. Fox is a good man, Melody."

Melody cleared her throat. "I can see that he is, but we're…we're taking things slow." As slow as they could considering he'd been inside her the night before, but they were doing their best to not talk about feelings or futures—a totally mature way to go.

As she watched her grandmother walk away, Fox came up behind her. She didn't have to look to know that he was near, she could feel the heat of him that went straight to her bones. He was just so…Fox. She couldn't explain it, and she wasn't sure she wanted to. She knew she should step away and keep her distance so they could talk about what would happen when the baby came. Because she didn't want to force him into a relationship, didn't want to force him into her life because of what had happened between them. They might have tried to be safe their first night together, but it hadn't been safe enough. And now, three lives would soon be changed irrevocably, forever.

"You looked like you were having a good time today," Fox whispered, the warmth of his breath sending shivers down the line of her neck. "And I noticed you practically taking notes on each person you saw. Do you need to write them down?"

She shook her head, turning in his arms though she knew she should pull away. Fox needed to know who she was, who she had been, if whatever was between them were to continue. Because there was another person who was part of them now, and she had to be far more careful than she had been when it came to Fox.

"I just saw first impressions and don't want to keep those as my only ones, but it's nice to finally put faces to some names." She bit her lip, doing her best to think about the party and not the fact that Fox was so close to her, the lean line of his body pressed along the side of hers so she could feel every inch of him.

And she meant every inch.

It scared her how quickly Fox had become part of her life. She'd thought they could be friends once she came back to Whiskey, but she should have known that wouldn't be the case. As evidenced by their first meeting, the sparks between them only flamed hotter once they were closer to one another for longer than a few moments. And the hell of it was, she *liked* him. He was amazing with his family, caring, funny, and always tried to show that he belonged with how hard he worked since his brothers were all so different. She could only assume that it would be the same if their sister were living there, as well. Fox was talented and had far more intricacies than she'd ever imagined. Things like his juggling when he was thinking, or the fact that he rambled just like her when he was nervous. He had made sure her grandmother was taken care of with his story, and though the editorial had gone viral, he'd made sure her family was safe from any prying eyes who wanted to know more about Ms. Pearl and her dancing past. Fox hadn't taken a step back and had only paused to let the fact that she was pregnant sink in before he was there for her, telling her that he wanted to be part of the pregnancy and part of the baby's life, even as they traversed their own relationship.

To say that she was confused when it came to her feelings about Fox was an understatement. But before she could let any sense of promise wrap itself around them, she had to tell him her secrets.

And because she knew she was being a coward, she couldn't let those secrets lie dormant any longer. Not when she knew the clock was ticking down when it came to what the two of them had made together.

Their child.

And there went that stomach roll again.

"Melody? You went quiet there." Fox slid his hand through her hair, tucking some behind her ear.

"Sorry, just thinking." She shook herself, letting out a breath. "I have a few things to clean up, but I wanted to say thank you for being here. I know you didn't have to be, but I appreciated it."

Fox cupped her face then and kissed her softly. The touch of his lips against hers went straight to her core, and she was thankful when he pulled away so she could think. That was the problem with Fox, she could never get her thoughts in order when he was around. And that was probably why she was pregnant and beyond confused.

"Of course, I had to. I know we're doing our best to not define what we are, but you've been in my bed, we talk and text for hours a day, and you're carrying my child. We're part of each other's lives, no matter what titles and labels we put on it."

"You're right," she said, obviously surprising him if the

look in his eyes was any indication. "Can I come over after this? There's a few things I need to tell you."

He gave her a curious look but nodded. "Let me help you clean up. The caterers did most of it, but there is probably a few things left I bet."

Relieved and nervous at the same time, she gave him her best smile that she had a feeling didn't quite reach her eyes. Fox was right in that there wasn't much to do, but she wanted the studio to shine since the real opening day would be right after the long weekend. Then she'd work with children and adults of all ages and practice and begin her new life once again. Since she wasn't actually dancing all day, she could work while pregnant for sure. She had seen previous instructors in that position, but it wouldn't be easy. Just another thing to add to her list. As long as she stayed organized and steady, she might not stress out to the point of getting sick again.

Fox was in the front of the studio, mopping the floors while Melody went out with the last of the trash bags. The caterers and Fox had cleaned up the heaviest of the mess so she didn't have to lift a lot, but there was still a tiny bag left that she wanted out of the building and into one of the cans outside. There was a slight chill in the air, but she didn't mind as she'd been slightly overheated with the amount of people at the party and being near Fox in general, but as she stared at what lay in front of the trash cans ice filled her veins.

"Melody? What's wrong? What the fuck is that?"

She swallowed hard. "Fox? I think you need to call the police. I think you need to now."

Because in front of the cans lay a single ballet toe shoe, the ribbons pristine yet splayed out above the shoe itself. But it was the drops of red, of what could be blood on the pink silk that told her that she'd been wrong before about the flowers. Wrong about the email and the note. Wrong about so much.

Someone was taunting her, stalking her, and she could only guess why.

Chapter 17

By the time the police came and left, Melody was frozen to the bone and Fox was stiff with anger beside her. She'd told the detectives about the email and the letter, as well as the flowers, and now this. When they pulled Fox away so she could tell the police in more detail *why* this could be happening in a new town, she'd told them the truth, and explained what had happened before she moved to Whiskey. She even gave them a list of who it could be, but for all she knew, it was someone totally different yet still connected to the time that had changed her life forever.

There hadn't been judgment in their eyes, but she could still feel it in her soul. When they left, taking the shoe with them, she hadn't wanted to stay at the studio any longer. She would come back since it was another part of her home, but that night, it felt tainted.

And when she found herself standing in front of her studio next to Fox, she wrapped her arms around her middle, waiting for what he would stay. Instead of asking her what was going on, he pulled her into his arms, and she sank into him, her body shaking.

"Let's get you to my place," he whispered softly. "The town's small, and they're going to wonder why the police were here. They won't know the details though, so let's call your grandma and make sure she knows. But I still want you with me. Can you do that? Can you give me tonight?"

She nodded, wiping away a tear that had broken through her control. "I can do that. I was planning on talking to you more tonight anyway."

His jaw tightened, and he gave her a nod. "Let's do it then."

She called her grandmother as he drove her to his place. She'd walked to her studio that morning since everything was in the building and she'd needed the air to calm down, but she was happy that he had his car just then.

When they were inside his house, each holding a cup of hot tea in their hands, she sat next to him on the couch and tried to figure out where and how to start.

"I want you safe, Melody. You don't need to tell me every secret, but I want to know why someone left a bloody ballet shoe behind your place, and why you had those flowers. I remember those even though you said they were nothing."

She set down her mug and faced him. "I was a ballet dancer. Though I guess you probably already knew that about me."

He set his cup down next to hers on the worn table before taking her hand and giving it a squeeze. He didn't say anything, just let her talk, and for that she was grateful.

"I had a natural talent. My mother did, too, just like Grandma Pearl. But while Grandma Pearl went to Vegas to be a showgirl as you know, my mother wanted to do something…classier." Melody rolled her eyes, remembering the fights the two women had gotten into over the years, their verbal sparring filled with love and sometimes a bit of bitterness that always coated her tongue. "So she went into ballet, but while she was a fantastic dancer, at least according to her, she didn't have what was needed to attend Juilliard, the height of her ambitions before going to dance for a company. So when she found herself with a little girl who loved to twirl, she put *all* of her energy into my dancing. Everything she had. And my father let her. He pushed me, as well, but it was different for him because he was the one who paid for things while Mom was the one who told me I *had* to be a dancer. If I didn't love dancing so much, I don't know what would have happened. But what *did* happen was that I let my stern parents who put their whole lives into shaping mine, and who told me over and over again that I had talent I couldn't waste…well, I let them turn me into someone I hated. Only I didn't hate that person at the time. I was the mean girl. The dancer who thought she was top shit, and no one could bring me down. Along with four of my friends—two girls, two boys—the five of us ruled the dancing world in our community and then at Juilliard."

Melody licked her lips, but when she considered stopping, Fox gave her hand another squeeze, and she was able to speak again.

"I wasn't a good person. I looked down on anyone in my way and below me. I thought that I could do no wrong. And one night before we were all set to leave school and go into our companies to rule the world, all five of us had far too much to drink. We were drunk, stupid, and because we thought no one and nothing could touch us, we drove."

She closed her eyes, the memories of what happened next slamming into her.

"I wasn't driving. I was in the back seat. Freddie was driving because he drove the best while drinking. The fact we even thought that makes me hate myself even more. Jake was in the passenger seat. Candice was to the right of me. And Sarah to the left."

"Oh, baby."

"You know what I said when we got into the car? I said, 'Oh, it's fine. We're not that drunk. We're fucking Juilliard dancers. Nothing can touch us right now.'" This time, tears fell, but she didn't brush them away, she deserved the shame.

"Freddie took a turn too quickly, and we rolled four times, hitting a pole. Freddie, Jake, and Candice died on impact. Sarah broke both her legs, a few ribs, and cracked her skull open." Melody let out a shaky breath. "I had a severe concussion, broke my wrist, and shattered my knee. Sarah's career was over. My career was over. And three of my best friends were dead because we thought we were better than everyone else and didn't have to follow the rules."

"Jesus Christ." Fox moved to wrap his arms around her, but she pulled away, shaking her head.

"Sarah never forgave me, and I don't blame her. Yes, she was drunk, too, but I ended up with the least scars. And I had been the one to say the words. The others' parents, families, and coaches put all of their blame on the two of us, and I left the area as soon as I could. There were no formal charges since we were legal drinking age, barely, and neither of us was driving, but I know what we deserved. I wasn't driving, but I let it happen because of my bad decisions. The choices I made helped kill three people and almost killed two more.

And we could have killed countless others with our recklessness."

"Melody, yes, you made the wrong choice, but you can't blame only yourself."

"You can say that, but I'm still going to. I can't help it. No amount of therapy and time will ever take that away. My parents practically disowned me once I was not only broken goods but also a stain on our family legacy. Mom died of cancer two years later, and Dad ended up dying of a heart attack far too young the year after that. I moved around for years, trying to figure out who I was while finding out if I could be the person I needed to be once I found a place to settle down to form roots. I'd thought Whiskey was that place. Hell, I thought maybe this whole baby thing was a way I could find roots with you." She hadn't meant to be that honest, but she was already baring the worst of her soul, she might as well come clean entirely. "Grandma Pearl doesn't look at me any differently for what I did, and I hope you don't either, but no matter what, I know that I'll have this child and always wonder what might have happened if my friends had been able to have children of their own. That will never go away. I need you to know why being with me could be a mistake."

Fox reached out and pulled her into his lap, his arms tight bands of steel that refused to let go. And because he kissed her softly, holding her as she let the tears fall once again, she let him cradle her, let him care for her, even if she felt as though she didn't deserve it.

"You're not a fucking mistake. You made one, yes, and you paid for it. And if whoever is threatening you is part of that, then you're still paying for that mistake. But we'll fix it. We can't bring them back, can't make it so you never get in that car, but we can make whoever is coming after you stop. I won't let you get hurt again. We all have parts of us who we aren't anymore. We've shed those past lives even within the few short years we get. I don't see the mean girl you spoke of. I see a woman who worked her ass off for her studio and didn't let a little thing like pregnancy derail her. You're working your ass off, and I'm so proud of you. I just wish you didn't have to go through that in order to find the woman you've become. And I'm not letting you go, Melody. Not now, and maybe not ever. I know we said no promises, but I think we're past that. Now let me hold you, and then we can figure out the next steps, but for now, just let me hold you."

So she let him hold her, let him try to soothe what she thought might never be fully comforted. And while she could fall into him in that moment, she knew she still had to be careful. Because he might know the facts, but time could change everything.

And she'd already lost everything once because of her wrong choices.

She couldn't lose it again.

Chapter 18

The next day while Melody stayed with her grandmother, Fox did his best not to start throwing things in stress and complete anger. He couldn't even pick up his normal things to juggle when he needed to think because he wanted to punch something and would probably end up throwing the balls at someone's head or something that could break.

He knew Whiskey had its issues. All towns did. Hell, his brother and Kenzie had almost been hurt by her ex-husband in Dare's bar, but he still couldn't believe someone was doing what amounted to *stalking* to Melody.

The police might have said they could handle it, but he wasn't sure he could leave her alone for long. He needed to be by her, needed to make sure she and the baby were okay. It didn't matter to him that he had to work and deal with his family; he just wanted to make sure that Melody was by his side and under his care. He knew it was overprotective, but someone was threatening the woman he was falling for, the woman carrying his child, and he didn't know what else to do.

Those at his work that morning had asked if there was anything to report about the police being called to Melody's after the party, but he'd dodged them just like the detectives. There was truly nothing to report, even in a small town where gossip was just as important to the town's perspective as the news. Thankfully, his staff seemed more worried about Melody than wanting answers that he didn't have.

He did, however, talk to his brothers and his parents about what had happened. He hadn't given them many details, as those were Melody's secrets to tell and not his, but at least the others now knew to keep their eyes open for anything that might seem out of place. Loch was already grumbling about adding new security to Ms. Pearl's home as well as to the studio itself. Fox was pretty sure the house already had top-of-the-line security thanks to Loch, but he wasn't going to argue. He just hoped that Melody and her grandmother didn't fuss.

He hated the fact that he couldn't be by Melody's side for most of the day, but he'd had to catch up on work, and she'd wanted to spend time with her grandmother. He and Melody had both been pretty shaky after they finished their conversation the night before, and while he knew she probably needed some space from him after she bared her soul, he didn't know if he would be able to give her as much space as she might think she needed.

Because the fact was, he was going to be a dad. He'd been so focused on doing the right thing and making sure that Melody knew she was cared for and wanted and that she wouldn't be alone in this, that he wasn't sure he was handling it the right way.

It worried him sometimes to think how focused he was on keeping Melody in his life and keeping her safe because he wanted to do the right thing when it came to their child. And then he reminded himself that he had wanted her as much as he did now before he knew she was pregnant. Given those two thoughts were so intertwined, he wasn't sure he could ever know exactly *how* he would've felt without the idea of the new life between them.

And while that worried him, he had a feeling it bothered Melody even more.

He'd never thought starting this new part of his life would be this way. He'd seen the way his brothers became fathers and had thought that maybe he'd be able to do something different. He'd thought that he would be able to have some semblance of control when it came to not only becoming a father but also starting a serious relationship. But it seemed, in the end, the Collins brothers only had one way of starting new parts of their lives. An insane way that never made any sense.

He was beyond stressed. Beyond worried. But in the end, he was falling for her so hard that it scared him. Especially because she was so hard to read. There was so much going on in her life that he worried he would be the easiest thing to cut out when she got too stressed and needed to focus on only the most important things.

And he hadn't known her long, but he knew deep down that he was falling for her. And that meant he was going to fight for her. She had been it for him since that first night, even if he had tried his best not to think about it. She had haunted his dreams when he thought he'd never see her again. And now, she filled his day when all he wanted to do was spend time with her and figure out every facet of her.

And he knew this intensity might scare Melody off, so he was going to do his best not to do that.

So tonight, instead of spending the evening with Melody, he was going to take the class that he had been signed up for for a while now. The one that probably made no sense to anyone looking in on him. But then again, sometimes, he felt as if no one knew what he was doing. Because he had spent his life being in the shadow of two amazing brothers, and one very talented sister. As his brothers had seemed to add on more jobs to their lives every day and even more twists and turns to their personal lives, Fox had been steady with his one job, and his routine when it came to working in his brother's bar some nights, and working out at his other brother's gym. So, of all things, he had signed up for a cooking class. He might as well be talented at something besides juggling.

His brothers were probably already better cooks than he was, but he didn't want to think those thoughts. Because he didn't like the jealousy that came with them. He wasn't envious of his brothers per se, but he always felt as if he had to work a little bit harder to match them. Because he looked up to them, looked up to Tabby even though she was younger, and he didn't want to be left stranded. He'd been left behind when it took him so long to fill out, and had felt slightly abandoned when the others knew what they wanted to do with their lives and Fox was still lost in his books.

But he wasn't that kid anymore. Now, he was going to have a kid of his own. So, yeah, this cooking class was for him, but he also knew that he would be able to cook for Melody and the baby when the time came. That was if he ended up part of Melody's life in the way he thought he wanted. Everything was so up in the air, and if he didn't stop and let things happen in their own way and time, he'd start pulling out his hair.

"You're staring at the sign and not actually walking into the building. Is there something I should know?" Ainsley hip-bumped him, and he shook his head, wrapping his arm around her shoulders. She might be Loch's best friend, but she was also his friend, and they'd decided to take the class together. She wanted to learn to be a better cook for herself and even for when she cooked for Misty, Loch's daughter. Fox thought she was already better than he was at cooking, though that wasn't saying much, even as their initial skill level assessment.

"Sorry, just thinking about nothing and everything, I guess."

Ainsley looked over her shoulder, presumably to ensure that they were alone when she whispered, "About Melody, the stalker, and the baby? It's a lot."

"Loch tell you about what happened?" He hadn't, but he wasn't surprised that she knew.

"Yes, but Melody also did when I called to make sure she was okay. I know I probably should have given her space, but she's my friend, and I'm nosy and invasive when it comes to my friends."

"That's what we love about you," Fox said honestly. "Now let's get to cooking before someone sees us out here."

They'd made a deal that they wouldn't let any of their friends know what they were doing. It was embarrassing to think that, at their age, they didn't have the basic skills to cook a normal meal, but they were learning. Somehow, the news hadn't gone through the grapevine of town gossip yet, and for that, he was grateful.

The class consisted of five pairs of students learning the basics of cooking and, eventually, how to put a full meal together that was a little bit fancier than normal. It was a ten-week course, and this was the second to last class. He had no idea how his parents and family hadn't figured out that he was taking the course, but he was just happy that he didn't have to deal with any questions. His mother would probably think it was all her fault that he'd had so much trouble even boiling water for such a long time, but at least he was getting better at it.

He and Ainsley were paired up, while most of the rest of the class was actual couples who were practicing for when they got married and started families, but he liked the fact that he was there with his friend and they could laugh about burning things and not making the most picture-worthy food ever.

Tonight, they were taking it easy with chicken Marsala and pasta. It sounded way too complicated for him, but what did he know. He'd only learned how to boil eggs correctly last month.

Ainsley was quiet beside him as she focused, and he liked that about her. She could talk a mile a minute when she wanted to, but she could also be the silent observer who was that steady rock for those around her when she needed to be. He knew his brother relied on her more than just for babysitting, and he had a feeling once Loch figured that out, things would change for the pair. He liked Ainsley, liked her for his brother, and really liked the fact that she was part of their lives. But when the two finally realized that they could be it for each other, Fox was afraid what might happen. His brother was even more bullheaded than Dare or himself, and if they weren't careful, they could all lose Ainsley because Loch was too afraid to trust.

The fact that it reminded him so much of Melody wasn't lost on Fox. He always trusted too easily, even for a writer, and he knew that. But he knew he wasn't putting that trust in the wrong hands when it came to the woman he wanted in his life. He might've fallen fast, but he didn't care. It wasn't just the baby, he reminded himself. It was the woman he wanted to know more, the one he didn't want to let go.

And that was just something they were going to have to deal with.

The class took around two hours to get through because they were also allowed to eat their food—if it turned out. Thankfully, between the two of them, they made a tremendous meal that filled his belly and made him want more. Maybe he would cook this for Melody one day since he knew she liked mushrooms. See? They knew little things like that. They weren't as new to each other as one might've thought without looking beneath the initial layer.

Now, he just had to make sure that Melody understood that, as well.

After he and Ainsley had cleaned up their mess, and it *was* a mess since neither of them was the cleanest of cooks, they headed out to make their way to their respective homes. Of course, because this was his life, nothing ever worked out the way he hoped. Loch and Melody were walking back from their businesses when they caught sight of Ainsley and Fox walking close together. Fox had been brushing flour off Ainsley's cheek and laughing because he was pretty sure he had been the one to put it there, when he noticed the other two across the street. Melody stood there with wide eyes, but he had no idea what she was thinking. Loch, on the other hand, glared at Fox's hand and turned on his heel to storm away.

Fox seriously had no idea what the fuck was going on in his brother's head. But that wasn't new. However, he was really worried about what was going through Melody's head at that very moment. He knew what the scene looked like, and he had just been telling himself that Melody had trust issues. He really hoped he hadn't fucked everything up.

Beside him, Ainsley sighed and whispered, "Because, of course." Then she looked at Fox and shrugged. "I guess the cat's out of the bag. But I think Loch is wrong about what kind of cat we're talking about. I would go chase him and explain, but I really don't care right now. I'm headed home. Thanks for a good class. Now go make sure your girl isn't thinking what Loch is probably thinking."

She kissed him on the cheek, aware that Melody was looking, and made her way to her car. Fox knew the other woman probably shouldn't have kissed him just then, but that was Ainsley. Always making sure that everyone knew exactly what was going on even if she had no clue about his brother.

Fox looked both ways before he crossed the street and made it to Melody's side. She had moved from where she'd been standing, though he was kind of annoyed that Loch had left her there alone, even though Fox had been close. But that was something he would have to deal with later since, right now, he wanted his attention only on the woman in front of him.

"So, it's not what you think." He winced. "And that's something any dude who's been caught red-handed says. But really, it's what I meant too. In an honest way."

Melody just rolled her eyes and patted her hand on his

chest. The fact that there was a smile tugging at the corners of her lips said it all, and he relaxed somewhat.

"Since Ainsley is totally in love with Loch even though she won't say it, and I don't even know if she knows…and Loch is totally in love with her even though he won't even dare to think it, I'm going with the fact that you were hanging out because you're friends. I'm not some shrew of a woman who automatically thinks cheating. And if Loch weren't so damn confused, even more confused than I am—and that's saying something—he'd have probably figured it out, as well. So, what were you two doing? And why wasn't I invited? Just kidding." She winked, and Fox fell that much more in love.

"We're taking a cooking class. We both swore we weren't going to tell anyone until we found some semblance of cooking talent because it's kind of embarrassing to still have to learn the basics at our ages. But we're getting better. And, somehow, the town hasn't ratted us out to the family. Or maybe my parents know and they're letting us pretend that we're keeping the secret. That's been known to happen since my mom always knows everything. As for what's going on between Loch and Ainsley? I have no clue, and I try to give them their space because things are a lot more complicated since there's a little girl involved. I just hope they can figure it out. And I'm really glad you didn't think I was cheating on you. Because you're my girlfriend, Melody, and I know we haven't talked about it, and we don't actually use titles, but I'm going to right now. You're it for me. I'm not going to stray, and I'll try not to keep secrets. That's the only secret I've been keeping, but still." He leaned down and took her lips, unable to hold back any longer. She smiled and kissed him back.

He was damn stressed about what was going to happen,

but he reminded himself that he also needed to live in the moment. And that meant he could live right then with his woman in his arms, her body pressed close to his.

When they broke apart, Melody still held onto his hand and looked up at him. "I need to head home because I promised Grandma that I wouldn't be out too late. She's worrying more than usual lately, and frankly, I don't blame her. But do you want to come with me? Unless you have other plans."

"That sounds like the perfect way to end the evening. I was going to ask if I could come anyway because we didn't get to spend much time together today, and I want to hear about your day. I'm glad it doesn't have to be by text."

She beamed up at him, and they headed to her car. Though she could walk from her house to the studio easily, they'd all agreed it would be better for her to drive or at least have someone with her at all times. Hence why Loch had been walking her to her car around the block. Fox had walked himself, so it was easy for him to just drive her car. Melody wasn't a fan of driving as it was, and he didn't blame her given her past, so she easily let him take the wheel.

By the time they got to her house, Ms. Pearl was getting ready for bed since she liked to spend the last hour of her evening reading and drinking chamomile tea with a face-mask. He loved hearing those little idiosyncrasies about the woman who had been the subject of his writing, as well as the woman who would help him be a part of Melody's life. Yes, he and Melody would have eventually found each other because of the baby, but he wasn't sure if it would have been the same if they hadn't tried to start their friendship—and then the relationship—because they met again at Ms. Pearl's house.

They talked with the older woman for a few minutes before she went upstairs, and that left Fox and Melody alone. Because heat danced between them, he didn't bother with the social niceties. He crushed his mouth to hers, needing to know that she was okay, needing to know that she was his—if only for this moment. Because she hadn't backed off when he called her his girlfriend, but she hadn't done anything else either. He was so afraid of losing her, and even with each kiss and brush of skin, he worried that they were getting closer and closer to their end.

He pushed that thought away, locking it firmly in a vault so he could focus on the woman in his arms.

"I want you. I've missed you."

She smiled against his lips. "I missed you, too. I don't know how I can crave you this much even though I just had you a few days ago."

"Too long." He kissed her neck. Her shoulder. "Let me take you upstairs. I promise we can be quiet."

She laughed, tilting her head so he could kiss her neck again. "No, we can't. Be quiet that is. But we're far enough away from Grandma's room that we can go upstairs and do what I've wanted to do all day. Make me feel, Fox. Make me yours. Okay?"

There was nothing he could do in answer except gather her up in his arms and kiss her again. He carried her to her room and closed the door behind them before he set her down on her feet, pressing her back to the hardwood of the door. She arched for him, a coy smile playing on her lips, and he couldn't help but take her mouth again. His hands roamed over her body, cupping her breasts, then caressing her belly for a mere instant before moving to her hips. They both seemed to notice the gesture, the fact that there was a life growing inside her part of their every waking moment. But right now, it was just about the two of them.

"I want to taste every inch of you. Take my time and lick and suck and bite. I swear every time together just gets hotter. It just makes me want you more." He sucked hard on her shoulder, pulling the strap of her top down so he could taste more of her. His cock ached, pressing into her hip, and it was all he could do not to strip them both right there and fuck her hard against the wall. But he wanted more, needed more than a hard fuck on a hot night. So he would take his time. Savor every inch of her. And maybe even pound into her because she rolled her hips and shoved right back every time he did.

"I think that sounds like a plan. But if you could suck my nipples right now, that would be great. Because they're aching for you and we're way too clothed at the moment."

Fox let out a sharp bark of laughter at that. He was always laughing when he was with her, even when both of them were so hot they were about ready to burst. So he did as she asked, slowly rolling her top up over her arms and head. Then he reached around and undid the clasp of her bra in one quick movement that had her eyes dancing, and slowly let it fall to the floor. The movement of lace and silk against what had to be her oversensitive skin was an erotic caress, even to him.

Her nipples were hard points, her breasts fuller than that first night. Her nipples had only gotten more sensitive with the pregnancy, and he loved it. He lowered his head, sucking one into his mouth, biting gently while cupping her other breast with his hand and stroking his thumb over her rigid nipple. And then he switched sides, loving the way she moaned, arching her back so more of her breast filled his mouth. He'd always been a breast man, and Melody had the perfect tits. Of course, he loved her ass, too. He loved when he stripped her pants down her legs just enough so they went under the globes of her butt so he could fuck her hard from behind and watch her curves juggle with each movement. He had to move back, catching his breath at that thought. Because Melody was just so damn hot, he was always afraid he would blow too early.

Before he could go to his knees and take down her leggings so he could play with her ass and her sweet pussy, Melody pushed him away and put her hands on his hips to switch their positions. He was so surprised and turned on by the action that he let her do it. Of course, the sight of Melody going to her knees in front of him meant that he would let her do just about anything just then.

She looked up at him, batting her eyelashes as she undid his belt and his jeans before pulling them down over his hips. He helped her, his cock springing free and bouncing against his stomach. He was that hard.

She took him in hand, giving him two pumps before licking the crown. His eyes crossed, and he fisted one hand in her hair, the other laid flat against the wood behind him so he didn't pull away and toss her to the floor so they could fuck each other hard. He loved the way she explored his length, licking and sucking down the hard line of him before going back to the head. She hollowed her mouth and danced her tongue along him before taking in the tip and sliding her tongue along the slit. She took her free hand and cupped his balls, rolling them in her palm as she bobbed her head, giving him the best blowjob of his life. And when she used her other hand to squeeze the base of him, he couldn't help but arch his hips and tug on her hair.

"Gonna come," he warned, but she didn't back away. Instead, she sucked harder, and when the first shot came from him, he called out her name, coming down her throat. He hadn't come that quickly since the first night when they had been drunk on whiskey and each other. And, frankly, he did not care.

Instead, he reached down, picked her up from underneath her shoulders, and brought his mouth to hers. He could taste himself on her tongue, and it just turned him on even more. She wrapped her legs around him, her leggings pressed against his dick so he had to somewhat waddle to the bed. He kicked off his jeans, then laid her on the bed so he could get to his favorite part. Well, at least *one* of his favorite parts.

He tugged on her leggings, loving the way that she played with her breasts as he stripped her down. Then he spread her legs and went to town, sucking and licking and eating her out. She tasted so damn good, and he wanted to feel her come on his face at least once, maybe twice before he was ready again to fuck her hard into the mattress. He sucked on her clit, humming, and she let out little puffy moans as she tried to catch her breath. He used one finger to play at her entrance, slowly working himself in and out of her as he readied her. Then he added a second and a third. He wasn't a small man, and he never wanted to hurt her. She was already wet for him, and not just from his mouth. And when he flicked his tongue over her clit and worked his fingers in and out of her with quick motions, she arched again and came, her sweetness filling his mouth.

As she lay there, catching her breath, he went to his jeans and slid on a condom. They hadn't had time to take their tests yet, and though he trusted her and she trusted him, they were still going to be safe just in case. Fox growled as he flipped her over onto her stomach, and she let out a giggle. He pulled her back so she was on the edge of the bed, her feet dangling off until they reached the floor. This was one of their favorite positions, and he really wanted to grab onto her ass and slide into her in one thrust. So that's exactly what he did. He slid in to the hilt, and they both moaned. She had enough curves that he could grab on tightly and fuck her hard. The best part was, though, that her toes dug into the carpet on either side of him, and she pushed back, thrust for thrust. She put her cheek down on the mattress, causing the rest of her to arch up even more so he could go even deeper. She was so damn hot this way, so damn his that he knew if he weren't careful, he would blow his load once again. Thankfully, her epic blowjob had taken off the edge so he could slide in a few more times and reach around to touch her clit. He only flicked her twice before she came again, squeezing his cock.

When she was still riding her high, he slid out of her, ignoring her moan because he missed the heat of her, as well, and rolled her onto her back—but not fully. Her legs were still to the side and pressed close together so he could slowly thrust in and out of her, working his way in inch by inch. The position made her even tighter, and she met his gaze, her eyes dark, and he knew they looked just like his just then.

He had one hand keeping her thighs together as he worked her, and the other went to her hand to tangle their fingers together. The position kept them so close, even though he wasn't hovering directly over her. There was nothing like it, and all he wanted to do was squeeze her hand and never let that contact go. Because of those thoughts, he thrust home once again, and they both came, their bodies shaking.

Melody was his, that much he knew. And it wasn't just the

sex. It wasn't just the way she made him feel in bed. It was because of everything she was.

And no matter what, he was going to do his best to make sure she knew that, even if she was scared of what they could have.

Chapter 19

Melody had so many feelings running through her, she had no idea how to organize them all so she could think. But she kept on about her day as normal since she was afraid that she'd either forget something or push *someone* away if she stopped.

Both were her go-tos when it came to stress and dealing with the aftermath of the accident, and while she might have thought it helped once, it really hadn't. So, instead, she found herself once again facing down the demons of her choices, but now she was afraid that she'd brought others into her pain, as well.

Melody stood in her studio, the quietness of the room almost deafening. Fox had left her alone to go get them something to eat from Dare's as she worked, though she knew Loch was close by, watching. The brothers never let her go anywhere, or at least not very far, without one of them near her since they were wound just as tightly as she was.

She was on the final stretch, just one more night until the

studio opened for her first dance class. While she was nervous, she was excited, as well. She'd put so much of her soul into this project, and now she would finally be able to what she'd dreamed of. Though the dream hadn't been one in her mind after the accident, it was still the one finally coming true.

No matter what, Melody would do her best not to let the past come back for her and ruin what she had in the present. Only it wasn't that easy, and she knew that whoever was leaving her those horrible *gifts* wasn't finished yet. She knew she deserved far more than a few broken bones from the accident. But, somehow, she'd thought that maybe she would find a way to live her life as it was rather than constantly having to look over her shoulder.

Apparently, she'd been wrong.

But she couldn't stop, couldn't let this rule her life. Not anymore. And she kept telling herself that so she'd believe it. What she needed to do was get out of her head, finish up the final details so she was ready for tomorrow's classes, and get home so she could relax with her grandmother and maybe even Fox if he stayed over again.

He was becoming so ingrained in her life, she knew she should worry, but with so much going on around her, it was hard to do that. She was falling for him, that much she knew. And while it should have worried her that everything was happening so fast, some part of her couldn't really get that. Because it wasn't as if they were in a normal relationship. They'd started off as a one-night stand that had turned to more and now was even greater than the two of them because they were having a baby. A small part of her worried that he was with her because of the baby and because he needed to protect her from whoever was after her—rather than because of what he felt for her inside. And she knew that was her own inner demons talking, but that didn't make the words wrong.

And because she would start to cry if she kept thinking about that, she let the words swirl out of her brain and sat at her desk to finish up the last emails for the day. The week prior, she had sent out reminder notices about what equipment and costumes her students would need to bring with them for their first day since those were already posted when they signed up. She knew dancing was a financial burden for many families, and she would never require the best of the best, but she also wanted to make sure that everyone was prepared. Tonight's email included a little bit more of that, as well as instructions for drop-off and pick-up times. While parents of the younger students would probably stay, she assumed that not everyone would be able to time-wise, and others would want to give their child space to learn.

Her mother had been at almost every single practice, a stage mom to rival all stage moms. She wouldn't say a word during the practices, but when they got home, she had plenty to say about Melody's ineptitude. She threw in sprinklings of how talented she had been and how much potential she had, but it always circled back to how Melody still had work to do even with her talent.

Melody would do her best to make sure her students were never put in that situation. It wouldn't be easy, and she would probably make mistakes, but that was something she was good at.

Emails done, she decided to at least stretch out a bit and dance something simple on her new floors to use all the nervous energy bubbling inside her. When she started showing as the pregnancy developed, she wouldn't be able to do this, but she at least wanted to keep her body in motion for now. She went to turn on her music and noticed a music box next to the sound system. Thinking it might be a gift from Fox, she bent down to open the lid. A soft melody began to play its chords, and it sent shivers down her spine.

She froze. That song…that familiar song.

Too familiar.

She had danced to it for hours with her friends, putting her sweat and her energy into fine-tuning it for their final program at Juilliard.

And she knew she didn't have the song on her phone currently because she'd never wanted to hear it again. She swallowed hard and looked down at the player, noticing that it was unplugged, but then again, that wasn't where the music was coming from. The haunting melody that would forever tighten its grip around her heart and soul was coming from her latest *gift*.

Someone was taunting her, and she was so damn scared.

Before she could look around and wonder if someone were watching her to get a reaction, the front door opened, and she screamed.

Fox dropped the bag of food and ran to her. "What's wrong?"

She didn't cry, but she did pull away from him, her hands shaking and her palms sweaty. "The music. I didn't choose that song. I didn't buy that music box. I thought maybe at first it was from you, but it couldn't be, could it? Because you don't know that song."

Fox's eyes widened before he glared at the music box. "How the hell did that get in here? Both doors were locked."

"But the alarm isn't on because I was sitting inside. Loch is going to update everything, but it's not done yet. Someone could have picked the lock or found a way inside to leave that there. I don't know, but we need to call the police. Because that's the song I danced with my friends to the night they died. That's the song we choreographed our final piece to as a group. There's no guessing what this could be connected to, not with that song."

Fox's hands on her shoulders tightened for a bare instant before he let her go, his fingers trailing down her arms to grasp her hands. She let him hold her there, knowing she needed to be strong. Because while she valued her safety and the safety of her unborn child, she also valued Fox's. What would've happened if he had been standing there when the person came in to bring the music box. Though more than likely, they had been watching the studio the whole time, waiting for her to be alone so they could drop it off. She would've noticed it when she first walked into the studio earlier that morning if it had been there overnight. At least she thought she would have. She didn't know, though, and that was something she would have to tell the police. But despite it all, she truly didn't want Fox to get hurt, and she was really afraid that's what would happen.

So after the police came and went, taking her statement once again and making her a spectacle of her new town, she put her hand on Fox's chest and let out a slow breath.

"What is it? I'm not going to let them hurt you. If that means I have to spend every single second by your side, I will."

She shook her head, knowing that wasn't the answer. Because in the end, she wouldn't let Fox be hurt. "That's not going to work, and both of us know it. I don't want you to get hurt, Fox. Maybe you need to give me some space. Because we both know that whoever's stalking me is watching you, too. They haven't hurt me yet, but what if they hurt you to get to me? I can't have that on my soul, Fox. I can't let you get hurt because of me. You mean more to me than I thought possible, and if we keep going like we are, you're going to get hurt. Maybe not by me. But by my past. I don't want that to happen, Fox. Please don't let that happen."

Fox's eyes widened before he took a step closer and ran his hand through her hair. "I'm going to let that pass because you're scared. And I'm going to take away the fact that you care about me more than you thought possible. It's something I'll always treasure. But I'm not going away. If you need space because I'm being overbearing? That I can do. But I'm not leaving you. Whoever is stalking you will have to go through me. And I know you hate to hear that, but for one moment of your life, let someone else take care of you. You are so damn strong, but let me take care of you. Let me take care of our baby. I know you're scared. Frankly, so am I. But we'll get better locks, and my brother can work on security. The police and the town are on the lookout for anything out of the norm. And with so many tourists, you might think that would be hard, but this town is smart. I'm here to take care of you. So don't push me away, Melody. I know you're smart and you're beautiful and you're scared, but don't push me away."

"Fox…" She didn't know what she might have said because there were no more words left. Because even though she wanted her space and wanted to push him away, she knew it wouldn't help anything. She had taken a chance on this man, and he wasn't letting her down. But with every breath she took, she felt as if she were the one letting him down.

"I can't let you get hurt."

"I can't let you get hurt either. So let's work together. Being apart and letting ourselves be alone for whoever this lunatic is won't help anyone. But if you need some space from me physically, where I'm not sleeping in your bed and holding you close, I can do that. I know we're moving pretty fast. But don't push me out of your life because of this person. Because in some aspects, it feels like that's what they want."

"Okay," she whispered, letting him hold her close after she'd spoken.

She hated the fact that this was happening at all. Because she was weak, because she didn't want to let Fox go even though she should, she let him drive her home after they had closed up the studio. Loch and his team were working hard on security before they opened tomorrow, but she was still worried that she was putting Fox and her students in danger because of her past choices.

The house was quiet when she walked upstairs, Fox right behind her. He went into her room to get his notebook that he'd left behind before they made dinner, and she went to her grandmother's room to say hello since the other woman hadn't come downstairs when Melody and Fox called out. That wasn't unusual, however, since her grandmother liked to take naps, and sometimes liked to read while drinking tea and got so engrossed in her story that she didn't hear the outside world.

Melody knocked softly on her grandmother's door. When there was no answer, she peeked her head in to make sure everything was okay. And then Melody screamed.

Chapter 20

"I'm fine. I just got a little dizzy."

Fox held back a snarl at Ms. Pearl's words since the other woman was currently laid out on her bed and looked anything but fine.

And because, no matter how long he lived, he would never forget the sound of Melody's scream.

Melody sat on her grandmother's bed after returning from the hospital, holding the other woman's hand and frowning. "A dizzy spell? I found you lying on the floor, your hand reaching out towards your phone, completely passed out. That doesn't seem like a dizzy spell. I can't believe I left you alone for so long. You were on the floor for two hours."

"I'm okay, baby girl. I promise. I just didn't eat enough today because I got involved in a good book and was so excited for your studio opening tomorrow. Don't you start to think that this is your fault. I know how much I need to eat every day because of my glucose levels. I'm a big girl, and I know what I'm supposed to do, and I didn't do it because I was stupid."

"Well, you're not going to do this again. If we have to write out everything and make a color-coded calendar or have a nurse in the house to force-feed you, we are not letting you get lightheaded again. Because the last time I was light-headed, I ended up pregnant." She winked as she said the last thing, forcing a laugh from Fox and Ms. Pearl.

"Yes, Melody. It's true. It must've been one of those gentlemen callers I still have. Me at the age of, well, I'm not going to tell you that, but you can probably guess. Yes, me at this age, having a baby. It's quite special. We can raise our children together."

Fox chuckled and went to sit in the chair behind Melody. That way, he could reach out and brush his hand along her thigh as Melody continued to talk to her grandmother. He didn't miss the warm looks Ms. Pearl gave him, but he figured since he was slowly becoming part of her life as he ingrained himself into Melody's, she would just have to get used to him being around.

"The doctor only let you come home and not stay overnight because your blood sugars were just a little off and everything else seemed fine. But that doesn't mean that Fox and I aren't going to watch you like hawks. I guess like foxes since that makes more sense with his name, but I digress. If you need anything, you call us. And we're going to seriously think about having a way for you to alert us or the hospital if you get in this position again. Because I love you, Grandma. You're my family, and I'm not going to let stupidity hurt us again. Do you understand?"

Ms. Pearl patted Melody's hand and nodded. "I do, my fierce protector. Now I'm going to sleep now that I've had all my food and beverages for the day. Tomorrow, after you get home from your classes, we can talk about exactly what needs to be done. Because I'm so glad you're back in my life, my favorite granddaughter. And I promise to take better care of myself. Because I am really ready to hold this great-grandbaby of mine. So make sure you take care of yourself, as well. And that means not letting any of the Collins boys out of your sight as they protect you from whoever is trying to hurt you and my great-grandbaby. Do you understand?"

Fox stood then and bent over the bed so he could kiss Ms. Pearl on the cheek. "I'll make sure she's safe. Because she's mine. Just like she's yours."

"You're a good boy, Fox. And I'm glad my Melody has you." When she patted his cheek, he couldn't help but smile. She looked so frail, a little older than she had the day before, but there was still a strength inside her, the same one he saw inside Melody. Ms. Pearl would be fine, at least for a few more years. And for that, he was grateful.

Melody didn't say anything as the two proclaimed what they were to her, but she did say goodnight to her grandmother and then walked side by side with Fox back to her room.

When the door was shut behind them, Fox held her close and kissed the top of her head. He hated seeing her like this, so scared and nervous. They hadn't had a lot of time to talk about what had happened earlier at the studio, but he knew it was on her mind. However, he had a feeling it wasn't what was at the forefront because of what happened with Ms. Pearl later. He was so damn lucky that she hadn't pushed through with the idea of keeping him out of her life for his own safety. Because he wasn't sure what he would do if he couldn't be near her at a time like this. Hell, he wasn't sure what he would do if he couldn't be near her at any time.

"I know you can't drink, even though today is the kind of day that deserves one, so I'm just going to hug you for a while and hope that's enough. If you want, I can use some of my newfound skills and cook something for you. I can't promise it'll be completely edible, but it will be the best I can do."

"I'm not really hungry. I'd like you to cook for me sometime, though. I don't think you're as bad as you say you are."

"You've never had my cooking. And I know you ate a big breakfast with me and nibbled on some things at the hospital while we waited to hear about your grandma, but that's it in terms of food. Just like you said with your grandmother, we need to make sure you eat enough, too. Because you're not just eating for yourself anymore, you know?"

"I know. But we did have that big breakfast, and I snacked all day. So I'm taking care of myself even if it's not that much fun right now." She went on her tiptoes and kissed him on the jaw. So he lowered his head and took her lips. He loved the taste of her, craved it. And he knew that no matter how many years he had with her, he would never get enough of her taste.

"You taste so damn good," he whispered against her lips. He knew he should stop with everything that had happened between the two of them, but when she deepened the kiss, he was lost and at her mercy.

"Make love to me, Fox? Make me feel good?"

He nipped at her jaw then ran his hands through her hair. He knew she loved that, and when she nuzzled into his hands, he held back a sigh of appreciation. He didn't speak, instead let his hands and mouth do the talking. He licked and sucked at her mouth, moving down so he could nibble at her neck.

She always shivered in his arms at that, and he knew it wasn't because she was ticklish. She craved his touch just as much as he craved hers.

He loved her. That much he knew. One might think it was too fast, but not between the two of them. His family fell hard and fast, and he'd seen it work in mysterious ways. But even though he loved her, he was going to wait to say it. Because she had so much going on in her life, he didn't want to add to the stress. But as he touched her and slowly stripped her out of her clothes, he had a feeling she already knew what he felt.

Fox had thought about his life and the fact that he'd been trying to find his place in his town and with his family. He had tried so many things. Tried to be the steady one. But, in the end, it seemed Melody might've been the one he was looking for the entire time. He didn't have to hide his love of writing and stories when it came to her. And though his family had never made him feel that way and had always honored and showed love for what he did, he had his own shortcomings when it came to self-esteem. Yet when it came to Melody, he didn't feel anything like that. She was his just as much as he was hers. And even though he wasn't going to say the words tonight, he planned to show her exactly how we felt.

He nipped at her nipples after he took off her bra, and she slowly ran her hands through his hair, her head falling back. Her long, blond hair flowed down her back, and she looked so much like a goddess right then he couldn't help but kneel at her feet. Then he pulled down her leggings and her underwear at the same time, placing a kiss on her mound before he helped her step out of her pants.

Melody moaned, spreading her legs for him. He grinned

and ran his thumb over her folds, using his other hand on her hip to keep her steady. Her pussy was already swollen, ready for his touch. And he knew she was sensitive there because she arched for him at just that barest graze of sensation. He slowly circled his thumb around her clit, teasing her. Then he twisted his wrist so he could use his two fingers to spear in and out of her as he paid attention to every breath and moan she made as he touched her. And when he lowered his head to her pussy and licked her swollen flesh, her knees went weak as she came. He grinned, using both hands to steady her as he stood up. Then he reached around and gripped her butt to pick her up in his arms. He loved that she was so small and compact even with all those curves. He could toss her on the bed pretty easily. But tonight, he wanted it to be sweet and all about her. Even though she reached for him, grazing her fingers along the long line of his erection beneath his pants, he pulled away so he could focus his attention on her and not himself.

He quickly stripped out of his clothes, rolled the condom over his length so he would be ready, and went back to feasting on her breasts. He always felt like he went straight to her pussy or her ass and sometimes forgot how beautiful her breasts were. And he didn't want her to forget either.

So he licked and sucked and molded them until she was panting and rocking her drenched core against his thigh. He could feel the heat of her on his skin, and it was all he could do not to thrust into her right then and there.

Then he rolled her over so he was on the bottom and she straddled him. "Put me in you," he whispered, his voice hoarse. "Ride me, Melody."

Her eyes were dark and filled with need, and when she reached down to grip the base of his cock and slowly slid herself over the length of him, his eyes rolled to the back of his head, and they both moaned. She rode him softly, rocking her hips as he slowly ran his hands over her body, cupping her breasts, squeezing her hips, sliding his thumb in and out of her mouth. She was the one in control, she was the one sending them both over the edge, and she was the one that he would love until the end of his days.

Chapter 21

Melody shouldn't be nervous, but she totally was. She might have made it through a whole week of dance classes with only a few hiccups, but that was nothing compared to this.

Tonight was dinner with Fox's family.

Meaning she would probably be interrogated and introduced as Fox's girlfriend.

Fox's *pregnant* girlfriend.

Dear God.

It wasn't as if they didn't already know she was pregnant. Hell, the entire town knew she was pregnant by this point because she was almost four months along and starting to get a tiny belly. She'd felt so guilty that she hadn't told all of her dance students ahead of time, that she waived their first fees if they wanted to cancel because she was pregnant. Somehow, nobody canceled, and she hadn't lost a single student yet. She might in the future, but for now, they were staying. Even though they knew she was pregnant.

And that meant no more hiding from Fox's parents, his brothers, or the women in their lives.

Hence why she was just a little bit stressed out and really worried that she was about to mess everything up by saying something stupid.

Fox, however, did not understand how she could be so stressed since she'd already met everyone. This was one area where he was a typical man and really needed to think before he spoke. But she didn't yell at him, afraid that if she did, she would start crying because her emotions were all over the place. She really didn't know if it was baby hormones or the stress of not figuring out who the stalker was that was making everything worse, but she was beyond tired of not knowing whether she was going to yell or cry any moment. And she wasn't even really that pregnant yet.

"It's going to be fine. My parents already love you from that one meeting and every time you come into the bar. You're giving the family tons of business, and they're already working with you at your studio. Yes, we went about this whole relationship a little backwards, but they're getting a grandbaby out of the deal, so I really don't think they're going to freak out about that. You don't have to worry either."

"You say that, and yet I'm walking in there pregnant and unwed. I might as well put on a shirt that is ruined or have a scarlet letter on my chest."

"As we are in a different century and Whiskey is a little more progressive than a lot of towns, especially compared Regency England, I'm going to go with no on the scarlet letter. But whatever you think is best."

"Sometimes you're very lucky that you're cute. That's all I've got to say."

Fox leaned over and kissed her hard. The touch left her pulse racing, and she had to fight to catch her breath. "Just cute? I'm going to have to step up my game when it comes to touching you if you just find me *cute*."

"Fox, keep your hands off that poor girl so she can come inside and actually get something to eat. Plus, she's carrying my grandchild; therefore, I want her sitting down with her feet up and a glass of ice water in her hand. For the love of Pete, Fox, keep your hormones at bay for at least five minutes."

That's it, Melody really needed to find that hole where she could bury herself and never actually think about what had just happened. Of course, his mother would be standing on the porch waiting for them. Of course, she would be staring and watching Fox make out with her as he made growling noises. And Melody was pretty sure she had made a moan or two of her own. Fox did that to her. Damn the man. Damn him and his pretty face and his yummy dick.

"Sorry, Mom. She's just so pretty." He gave Melody a wink before taking her hand and leading her towards the house. Fox's mom rolled her eyes before opening her arms for a hug.

"That boy is just too smooth for his own good. Or at least he thinks he is. I know we've already met, but just in case you forgot, I'm Barbara. Bob's inside, chasing the other two grandkids around the house. I don't know exactly what game they're playing, but it makes the kids giggle, and it keeps them out of the kitchen so they're not pilfering food. Keeping my children out of the kitchen, well…that's just never going to happen."

All of her nervousness seeped out of her at Barbara's hug. Because not only did that woman give good hugs, she immediately made Melody feel at home. And though Melody had met every single person inside the house, Fox's mother introduced her to everyone again and then literally sat her on the couch, put her feet up on the ottoman, and handed her a glass of ice water.

Kenzie laughed at the expression on Melody's face. "Let her take care of you. The boys keep pushing her away, and now that Tabby has decided to stay in Denver, she needs someone to pamper."

"She's still pampering you," Dare said as he walked into the living room with two glasses of iced tea in his hands. He handed one to Kenzie and sipped the other. Melody remembered that Dare was working that night at the bar, hence why he wasn't having a beer like Fox and Loch were.

Fox's father was indeed chasing Nate and Misty around, the noise almost deafening, but no one said anything. The three of them were having a blast, or at least Melody thought a good time was had by all. Loch was fixing a hinge on a door to one of the rooms down the hall but was still in the middle the conversation between Dare, Fox, and Kenzie. Melody tried to keep track of it all but still felt two steps behind. It didn't help that she was already getting pregnancy brain and was a little too tired to be on her feet. Fox's mom really knew what she had been talking about with putting her feet up.

Barbara wouldn't let most of them in the kitchen to help out with food since she had her own way of doing things, but Fox had told Melody that wasn't always the case. Sometimes, his mom was just in the mood to cook and perhaps work with one person.

That person today happened to be Ainsley. Apparently, Ainsley was doing even better than Fox at the cooking class, and Barbara wanted to see what the other woman had learned. Every once in a while, Misty would come up to Ainsley, give her a hug, and then go running after Nate. Melody knew she wasn't the only one who saw that interaction; the rest of the family watched it as well, but they all seemed to be doing their best not to say anything.

Because whatever was going on between Loch and Ainsley was none of their business, even though she had a terrible thing feeling that things wouldn't end well if the two of them didn't talk to one another. But knowing Loch as she did, talking wasn't going to come easily or anytime soon.

Melody rested her hand on her belly and let out a sigh. Fox had his arm wrapped around her shoulders and kissed her forehead. He didn't say anything to her, and he didn't need to. She could feel his comfort and his need, especially since it matched her own.

She was going to be a mom, that much had finally gotten through her head. Fox was going to be a dad. It should have stressed her out more than it did, but with everything else, it was just about par for the course. It was going to be something completely different, something else that would change their lives forever.

But Fox's family surrounded her, and she was comforted by the fact that she knew her grandmother was hanging out with her friends tonight and wouldn't be alone. Fox had been by Melody's side throughout it all and hadn't backed away—even when she tried to push him. She saw the strength in Bob and Barbara's love and marriage. She saw a similar strength in Dare and Kenzie's relationship. She saw the laughter from Misty and Nate. And she saw the delicate temptation between Loch and Ainsley. All of that surrounded her and reminded her that she wasn't alone. As she leaned into Fox, Melody figured that maybe just this once, she could trust herself. She could trust him.

Maybe this feeling she had wasn't wrong. Maybe she was finally falling.

Maybe she'd already fallen in love.

Chapter 22

Melody was actually smiling. Not just smiling, practically skipping. She'd finished her morning barre class with some amazing women who wanted a different way to work out than the gym next door, and now her belly was full of some amazing food thanks to Dare's bar. Kenzie had taken the afternoon off, and it was a teacher workday, so Ainsley was off, too, and the three them had eaten to their hearts' content. Or rather, her belly's content.

She'd gorged herself on a double cheeseburger with mushrooms and onion rings on the side. The girls and she had even shared some artichoke and spinach dip with some of the best homemade chips she'd ever had her life. She knew she'd work off the really bad food later on that day, or she probably wouldn't have indulged as much as she did. But what she really wanted to do was go to the back of the bar and meet Dare's chef and thank him for the amazing food.

Apparently, being pregnant had suddenly catapulted her into someone who couldn't help but try every single thing on the menu. Fox had even cooked for her the night before, and he hadn't burned a thing. Yes, it had been grilled cheese and tomato soup, but the soup hadn't been from a can. And for some reason, she had never been able to make grilled cheese herself. No matter what she did, she either added too much butter or ended up burning it. Or worse, she flipped it too fast, and the bread got all mushy, and there was cheese everywhere. So, in her mind, Fox was a very talented chef, but she planned to beg him to take her out for onion rings more often.

If she weren't careful, her baby would have the middle name "onion rings" considering how many she'd eaten in the past month she lived in Whiskey.

Things had quieted down around them, and she and Fox were actually starting to form a relationship beyond what they should have been, or rather what they *thought* they should've been. She'd fallen in love with him, and she knew she needed to find the guts to actually tell him that. It shouldn't have been scary, not with how many other scary things she had gone through in her life. How many other things she was *still* going through.

Her dance studio was thriving, and her students were adorable and hard-working even if sometimes they didn't want to stretch or plié. She didn't mind though, because she was learning along with them. Some of her older students were far more talented than they gave themselves credit for, and she was excited to start working with them one-on-one. And she'd already started putting feelers out for someone to take over the studio when she needed time to recover from having the baby.

Because though she'd been hiding from her past for far too long, she really did know a lot of people in the dancing world. And not everybody hated her as much as she hated herself.

And because that thought had entered her mind, she couldn't help but wonder where the stalker had gone. It'd been two weeks since the music box showed up. Two weeks, and she hadn't heard anything from the person who was trying to make her worst fears come true. The police felt helpless, trying to figure out how any of it had happened, but there just wasn't evidence. Melody was never alone now, one of the Collins brothers or her friends were constantly around her.

It should have annoyed her, should have been claustrophobic, but she let them take care of her, and it made Fox happy. And making him happy was something Melody wanted to do.

She'd never been good at relationships. But now, Fox was part of her life, and maybe tonight over another plate of onion rings, she would finally tell him exactly what was in her heart.

Because she loved him, and it was past time she told him. And the thing was, she wasn't scared that he didn't love her, too. Because it was in each and every one of his actions. But she knew he was waiting for her to say the words because she needed to be the one to say them first. It was how they were and she appreciated that.

And, oddly enough, she didn't mind.

"You have a dreamy look on your face, and you totally just missed Kenzie saying goodbye because she had an emergency upstairs. Probably just a towel issue, but those are big things when it comes to innkeeping."

Melody winced at Ainsley's words and offered the last onion ring as an apology. "Sorry."

"It's okay, I know you're thinking about your dreamy Fox and how handsome and manly and growly he is. But you're going to see him later, so you can keep your sad little onion ring while I walk you back to your studio. I figured I'd hang out with you if that's okay. I really don't want to go home and grade. So I figured I'd smile and be happy watching little girls in tiny tutus prance around while you do your best to be stern."

"That sounds like a plan because, honestly, I wouldn't want to grade either. It's too nice of a day."

The two of them made sure that they tidied up their mess and left a big tip since this was turning out to be their second home. Or maybe it was a third home at that point. They waved at Dare, and he waved back from where he stood behind the bar, and then she and Ainsley made their way outside and into the street where they could walk to the studio. She'd truly fallen in love with the town. Every single person had opened his or her arms to her, and she never once felt like a tourist. They'd helped her build her dreams, and had helped her feel safe when she didn't think she could. No, they didn't know her past, but they didn't ask either. For such a curious and gossip-filled town, they truly held back when it came to the important things.

She was just waving to the barbershop owner, a very hunky guy with a nice beard that happened to rival any of the Collins brothers' when the sight of the car coming up pretty fast on the road stopped her.

Ainsley was closest to the curb, but Melody was right there beside her. The car sped up, and somebody screamed. Ainsley held onto Melody's arm, but Melody pushed the other woman out of the way. The car jumped the curb and slammed into the pole right where Ainsley had been standing, and right in front of Melody. Another scream pierced the air, and Melody fell back, her head slamming into the pavement. She rolled to her side, protecting and cradling her belly. Ainsley was on her knees in a second, and others crowded around her. But she didn't really hear any of it, she could only think about the baby in her belly beneath her hands. And the fact that Fox wasn't beside her, watching her every move. He would blame himself for this.

But it wasn't his fault.

It was the fault of the woman behind the wheel.

The woman that Melody should've known was part of this all along.

The woman that Melody had helped to ruin. Because she would know Sarah's face anywhere.

Chapter 23

Once again, Fox found himself standing in a hospital room, looking down at someone he cared about. He'd done it for Ms. Pearl only two weeks ago, and now he was looking down at the mother of his child—the woman he loved. He couldn't believe that a fucking car had almost hit her. Yes, she was going to be okay, but a car had almost hit her.

That didn't happen in Whiskey. Even with all the tourists and cars on their tiny roads, people didn't get hit by them.

But, apparently, the love of his life did.

Melody told him not to blame himself, but he was going to, at least a little bit. Sarah had found out where Melody was because of his viral news story. Because Sarah had learned of Ms. Pearl long before his article ever reached the internet, and she had known exactly who was related to the woman who danced for the Rat Pack and possibly the mob. The woman had used that and Fox's details to find out where Melody was so she could take out her sick revenge on her. Sarah wasn't a dancer anymore. And, apparently, seeing Melody dance even as an instructor had been too much for her. So she'd broken and tried to break Melody in turn.

"If you keep pacing and beating yourself up over this, I'm going to get out of this bed and smack you upside the head. Don't make me get up when the doctor told me to lay down for just a little bit. Come over here and hold my hand."

Fox glared at the love of his life and held back the bitter retort that he wanted to say. It wasn't her fault that she'd gotten hurt. None of this was her fault. And she had told him more than once that this wasn't his fault either. It didn't make the pill he had to swallow any less bitter.

"I'm fine, Fox. Please, just stop pacing. I don't have a headache, but you are about to give me one. The doctors didn't even put me in a gown. I'm still wearing my clothes."

"I can see you're wearing your own clothes because I can see the hole at the elbow where you scraped yourself when you fell down. There's a bandage under that hole. I can see the white of it. Don't tell me that you're fine when you were clearly bleeding earlier." But he did stop pacing and went over to her side. And then he sat down right on the edge of the bed and held her hand, lowering his head so he could press his forehead to hers.

"Fox, baby, I'm fine. Yes, it was scary. Sarah is behind bars and, hopefully, she'll get the help she needs. I knew it either had to be her or someone else close to the accident. When I told the police her name after the ballet slipper incident, they said they were going to look for her. It hurt me at first because I didn't want to encroach on her life any more than I already had, but I had no idea where she was. I haven't heard from her since right after the accident when she yelled at me. Yes, I know she was drunk, too, but I was the leader, and I failed."

This time, Fox did growl after kissing her hard on the mouth. "You did not fail. You made a mistake. But so did she. But did you go and stalk her like an insane woman? No. Sarah is disturbed, and she could've hurt you. The only reason she's the one with the concussion is because she hit a pole instead of you or Ainsley. She could've hurt way more people than that." He cupped her face, holding her close. He knew his hands were still shaking after being so close to losing her, but he didn't care. She needed to see the breadth of his emotions, the depth of what he felt for her. Because that wouldn't change anytime soon. He'd fallen in love with Melody, and it was past time the told her.

"And she won't be able to hurt anyone else or herself again. I'm okay, Fox. That part is over. Now, we only get to look at the future. Right?"

There was a slight uncertainty in her tone that worried him. But he hoped it was just because of the adrenaline fading after the accident.

"Right."

She let out a breath, and a small smile appeared on her face "You know, I was going to wait until tonight when I ordered some onion rings and we could munch on them together, but I figure this could be the perfect time."

"You and your onion rings," he murmured, earning him a smile.

"Don't knock them. But what I wanted to tell you tonight was that I love you. I love you so damn much it's scary. I think I started falling for you that first night we drank too much whiskey. When we created our baby together. I don't know what will happen in the future, but I do know that our lives will be forever intertwined because of this child. But I don't want our lives to be connected just because of him or her. I want us to be connected because I love you. And it didn't take someone behind the wheel of a car trying to hurt me for me to figure that out. I knew before, and I think it's time you know."

This time, it was Fox who got choked up. "You stole my thunder, baby. I was finally going to tell you that I love you tonight. Only over grilled cheese instead of onion rings." She licked her lips, and he laughed. "We can still have both tonight. But, Melody? I love you so damn much. You're it for me. I love your strength, your tenacity, your talent, your beauty, your brains, and the fact that you make me smile. I love that you make my family happy, and you're forever trying to make sure that everybody's included. I just love you so damn much. And I should have told you before this, but right now, with you in my arms looking at me like that, I guess it's the perfect time."

And then he kissed her, not able to hold himself back. He had one hand on her belly, her fingers tangled with his, and the other in her hair as he kissed her. He was sure the doctor was going to come in any moment, or maybe the rest of his family to check on them. But he didn't care. He had the woman he loved in his arms, and that was all he needed. After searching Whiskey for far too long, he'd finally found exactly what made him Fox.

Epilogue

Fox's fingers dug into Melody's hips as he thrust into her wet heat. Her pussy was so hot, so wet, that he slid home right to the hilt. This was the first time without a condom, and going bare was possibly one of the best moments of his fucking life.

Melody arched for him, and he wrapped her hair around his fist so he could fuck her hard into the mattress. She panted, calling out his name, and he did the same with hers. He loved viewing her from this angle. Loved the way the curves of her ass just enveloped his cock. She was so damn hot, and one day, he was going to marry her. They were going to wait until after the baby was born, even though that might not be what others thought they should do. But they wanted to wait and do things on their own terms, even if it was backwards.

And that meant he still had a few months to bang his girlfriend rather than his wife. The last time he had said that,

Melody had slapped him upside the head and then gave him a blowjob.

They were officially crazy for one another.

Melody's inner walls clamped around him, and she came. He pulled out quickly and flipped her over to her back so he could slide into her one more time. Neither of them could catch their breaths as he hovered over her, crushing his mouth to hers as he pounded into her as hard as he could. He loved it when they were slow, the build-up tantalizing, but he loved it even more when they went hard and fast. Melody's fingernails scraped down his skin, and he knew he would have marks later on. And he loved it. Loved her. He slid his hand between them and played with her clit, and when she came again, this time, he filled her up.

They were sweaty, wet, and a little sticky, but he honestly never wanted to get out of bed.

"I think that was a good way to see if we really like morning sex with you living here." Melody laughed and ran her hand over the swell of her stomach. She was just now starting to show a little bit more, but they had a long while until the baby was born.

That would give them more time to get to know each other fully, inside and out. And time to make up a nursery in Ms. Pearl's home. Fox had moved in the week before, knowing that neither of them wanted to leave the older woman alone. Fox didn't mind renting his house out for a bit. After all, he'd fallen in love with the home, Ms. Pearl, and Melody, all in quick succession.

"I think morning sex is a win," he agreed, kissing her softly. "But I'm sure your grandma heard us."

She blushed. "Well, I'm sure she's heard worse."

He kissed her again, holding her close. He'd never

thought that this was how his life would turn out, and yet, in the end, it seemed as if it was the perfect way for it to happen. He'd fallen in love with a dancer, a woman who never left his mind, even when he'd thought she should. He was going to be a father, and was so damn excited to watch Melody be a mother. His family had taken her in and hadn't once questioned the track that Fox and Melody were on.

Because that's what his family did. They took people in and always made sure they were safe and well loved.

And as he held his future wife in his arms, knowing they both needed to get out of bed since he had another project to work on and she had a dance class in a couple of hours, he knew that today was yet another start to what would be the rest of their lives.

And to think, it had all started with one shot of whiskey too much, and a temptation smooth as sin.

Coming next...Loch and Ainsley finally get their book in Whiskey Undone.

A Note from Carrie Ann

Thank you so much for reading **WHISKEY REVEALS**. I do hope if you liked this story, that you would please leave a review! Reviews help authors *and* readers.

I hope you loved Fox and Melody as much as I do. Their story took some twist and turns and made me so happy! And I LOVE the fact that it's set in the same world as my Montgomerys so there's always a few surprises for longtime readers!

Don't miss out on the Montgomery Ink World!

- Montgomery Ink (The Denver Montgomerys)
- Montgomery Ink: Colorado Springs (The Colorado Springs Montgomery Cousins)
- Gallagher Brothers (Jake's Brothers from Ink Enduring)

- Whiskey and Lies (Tabby's Brothers from Ink Exposed)

If you want to make sure you know what's coming next from me, you can sign up for my newsletter at www.CarrieAnnRyan.com; follow me on twitter at @CarrieAnnRyan, or like my Facebook page. I also have a Facebook Fan Club where we have trivia, chats, and other goodies. You guys are the reason I get to do what I do and I thank you.

Make sure you're signed up for my MAILING LIST so you can know when the next releases are available as well as find giveaways and FREE READS.

Happy Reading!

The Whiskey and Lies Series:

A Montgomery Ink Spin Off Series

Book 1: Whiskey Secrets

Book 2: Whiskey Reveals

Book 3: Whiskey Undone

Want to keep up to date with the next Carrie Ann Ryan Release? Receive Text Alerts easily!

Text CARRIE to 24587

About Carrie Ann

Carrie Ann Ryan is the New York Times and USA Today

bestselling author of contemporary and paranormal romance. Her works include the Montgomery Ink, Redwood Pack, Talon Pack, and Gallagher Brothers series, which have sold over 2.0 million books worldwide. She started writing while in graduate school for her advanced degree in chemistry and hasn't stopped since. Carrie Ann has written over fifty novels and novellas with more in the works. When she's not writing about bearded tattooed men or alpha wolves that need to find their mates, she's reading as much as she can and exploring the world of baking and gourmet cooking.

www.CarrieAnnRyan.com

More from Carrie Ann

Montgomery Ink: Colorado Springs

Book 1: Fallen Ink
Book 2: Restless Ink (Coming Aug 2018)
Book 2.5: Ashes to Ink (Coming Jan 2019)
Book 3: Jagged Ink (Coming Feb 2019)

The Whiskey and Lies Series:
A Montgomery Ink Spin Off Series

Book 1: Whiskey Secrets
Book 2: Whiskey Reveals
Book 3: Whiskey Undone (Coming Oct 2018)

The Fractured Connections Series:
A Montgomery Ink Spin Off Series

Book 1: Breaking Without You (Coming Apr 2019)
Book 2: Shouldn't Have You (Coming May 2019)
Book 3: Falling With You (Coming July 2019)

Montgomery Ink:

Book 0.5: Ink Inspired
Book 0.6: Ink Reunited
Book 1: Delicate Ink
Book 1.5: Forever Ink
Book 2: Tempting Boundaries
Book 3: Harder than Words
Book 4: Written in Ink
Book 4.5: Hidden Ink
Book 5: Ink Enduring
Book 6: Ink Exposed
Book 6.5: Adoring Ink
Book 6.6: Love, Honor, & Ink
Book 7: Inked Expressions
Book 7.3: Dropout
Book 7.5: Executive Ink
Book 8: Inked Memories
Book 8.5: Inked Nights
Book 8.7: Second Chance Ink

The Gallagher Brothers Series:

A Montgomery Ink Spin Off Series

Book 1: Love Restored
Book 2: Passion Restored
Book 3: Hope Restored

The Talon Pack:

Book 1: Tattered Loyalties
Book 2: An Alpha's Choice

Book 3: Mated in Mist
Book 4: Wolf Betrayed
Book 5: Fractured Silence
Book 6: Destiny Disgraced
Book 7: Eternal Mourning
Book 8: Strength Enduring (Coming July 2018)
Book 9: Forever Broken (Coming Jan 2019)

Redwood Pack Series:
Prequel: An Alpha's Path
Book 1: A Taste for a Mate
Book 2: Trinity Bound
Book 2.5: A Night Away
Book 3: Enforcer's Redemption
Book 3.5: Blurred Expectations
Book 3.7: Forgiveness
Book 4: Shattered Emotions
Book 5: Hidden Destiny
Book 5.5: A Beta's Haven
Book 6: Fighting Fate
Book 6.5: Loving the Omega
Book 6.7: The Hunted Heart
Book 7: Wicked Wolf

The Branded Pack Series:
(Written with Alexandra Ivy)
Book 1: Stolen and Forgiven
Book 2: Abandoned and Unseen
Book 3: Buried and Shadowed

Dante's Circle Series:
Book 1: Dust of My Wings

Book 2: Her Warriors' Three Wishes
Book 3: An Unlucky Moon
Book 3.5: His Choice
Book 4: Tangled Innocence
Book 5: Fierce Enchantment
Book 6: An Immortal's Song
Book 7: Prowled Darkness

Holiday, Montana Series:
Book 1: Charmed Spirits
Book 2: Santa's Executive
Book 3: Finding Abigail
Book 4: Her Lucky Love
Book 5: Dreams of Ivory

Stand Alone Romances:
Finally Found You
Flame and Ink
Ink Ever After

Fallen Ink

From New York Times Bestselling Author Carrie Ann Ryan's Montgomery Ink: Colorado Springs series

FALLEN INK

Adrienne Montgomery wasn't going to throw up, but it would probably be a close call. It wasn't that she was a nervous person, but today of all days was bound to test her patience and nerves, and she wasn't sure if all those years of growing a spine of steel would be enough.

Maybe she should have worked on forming a steel-lined gut while she was at it—perhaps even a platinum one.

"You're looking pretty pale over there," Mace said, leaning down low to whisper in her ear.

She shivered involuntarily as his breath slid across her neck, and she looked up into her best friend's hazel gaze. The damn man was far too handsome for his own good, and he *knew* she was ticklish, so he constantly spoke in her ear so she shivered like that.

She figured he'd gotten a haircut the day before because the sides were close-cut so you could see the white in his salt-and-pepper hair. He'd let the top grow out, and he had it brushed to the side so it actually looked a little fashionable rather than messy and just hanging in his eyes like most days. Knowing Mace, he'd done it by accident that morning, rather than making it a point to do so. Her best friend was around her age, in his thirties, but had gone salt-and-pepper in his late twenties. While some men might have started dying their hair, Mace had made it work with his ink and piercings—and the ladies liked it.

Well, at least that's what Adrienne figured. It wasn't as if she were one of his following. Not in that way, at least.

"Yo, Adrienne, you okay?"

She glowered, hearing the familiar refrain that had been the bane of her existence since she was in kindergarten and one of the fathers there had shouted it like the boxer from that movie she now hated.

"What did I say about using that phrase?" She crossed her arms over her chest and tapped her foot. She was at least six inches shorter than her best friend, but since she was wearing her heeled boots, she could at least try to look intimidating.

Mace being Mace just shrugged and winked, giving her that smolder that he'd practiced in the mirror after seeing *Tangled* with her years ago. Yeah, he was *that* guy, the one who liked to make her smile and knew she had a crush on the animated Flynn Rider.

"You know you like it." He wrapped an arm around her shoulder and gave her a tight squeeze. "Now, are you okay?

Really? Because you honestly look like you're about to throw up, and with the place all new and shiny, I don't know if vomit really sets the tone."

Thinking about the reason the place—*her* place—was all new and shiny sent her stomach into another roll, and she let out a long breath.

"I'm fine."

Mace just stared at her, and she kicked his shoe. Mature, that was her name. "Try it with a little more enthusiasm, because while I'd *like* to believe you, the panic in your eyes doesn't really portray the right confidence."

"I'll *be* fine. How's that?" she asked and gave him a wide smile. It must have looked a little manic, though, since he winced. But he gave her a thumbs up.

"Okay, then. Let's get out of this office and go out into your brand new tattoo shop to meet the horde."

There went her stomach again.

Her tattoo shop.

She couldn't quite believe it. After years of working for others in Colorado Springs instead of going up north to Denver to work at her cousins' shop, or even south to New Orleans and her brother's former shop, she was now part-owner of Montgomery Ink Too, the first offshoot of the main shop in downtown Denver.

Yep, she was going to be sick.

"It's mostly family. Not quite a horde." Sort of, at least. Even three people felt like a lot at this point since they'd all be there…waiting for her to say something, do something, *be* someone. And that was enough of that, or she really wouldn't make it out of the office that day.

"True, since most of your family didn't come. The entire

Montgomery clan would probably fill four buildings at this point."

"You're not wrong. Only Austin and Maya came down from Denver since Shep and I asked the others to stay home. It would be a little too much for our small building if everyone showed up."

"But your sisters and parents are here, plus Shep and his wife, of course, and I'm pretty sure I saw their baby Livvy out there, too. And then Ryan, since you hired him." Mace stuffed his hands into his pockets. "It's one big, happy family, who happen to be waiting for you to go out there and possibly start a tattoo a bit later for your first client."

After what had seemed like months of paperwork and construction, today was opening day for Montgomery Ink Too—MIT for short. Ryan and Mace had called it that one day, and the nickname had stuck. There was nothing she could do now but go with it, weirdness and all. There had been delays and weather issues, but *finally*, the shop was open. Now, she needed to be an adult and go out into the main room to socialize.

And there went her stomach again.

Mace's strong arms came around her, and she rested her head on his chest, tucking herself under his chin. He had to lift his head a bit so she could fit since she wasn't *that* short, but it was a familiar position for them. No matter what anyone said about Mace, he gave *great* hugs.

"You're going to be fine." His voice rumbled over her, and she could feel the vibrations through his chest and against her cheek.

"You say that now, but what if everything tumbles down and I end up with no clients and ruin the fact that Austin and Maya trusted me with their first satellite shop."

Austin and Maya were two of her numerous Denver cousins. There were eight freaking siblings in that family, and all of them had married off—with Maya having *two* husbands even—so it added up to way too many people for her to count. Maya and Austin owned and operated Montgomery Ink in downtown Denver—what was now the flagship shop it seemed.

Her cousins had come to her over a year ago, saying they were interested in expanding the business. Since real estate was sparse off the 16th Street Mall where Montgomery Ink was located, they'd come up with the idea of opening a new tattoo shop in a different city. And wasn't it nice that they had two other artists in the family so close? Well, Shep hadn't actually been close at the time since he was still living in New Orleans where he'd met his wife and started his family, but now her big brother was back in Colorado Springs and was here to stay.

Maya and Austin were still the main owners of the business and CEOs of the corporation they'd formed in order to add on, but Shep and Adrienne had bought into the franchise and were now partial owners *and* managers of Montgomery Ink Too.

That was a lot of responsibility on her shoulders, but she knew she could do it. She just had to buck up and actually walk into the tattoo shop.

"Stop freaking out, Addi. I wouldn't have come with you on this journey if I didn't believe in you." He pulled away and met her gaze, the intensity so great that she had to blink a few times so she could catch her breath.

He was right. He'd given up a lot for her. Though, in the end, the whole arrangement might work out better for him. Hopefully. He'd left a steady job at their old shop to come and work with her. The trust in that action was staggering, and it gave Adrienne the final bit of strength she needed to do this—whatever *this* was.

"Okay, let's do this."

He held out his hand, and she took it, giving it a squeeze before letting go. It wasn't as if she needed to brace herself against him again or hold his hand as they made their way into the shop. Enough people already wondered just what went on behind closed doors between the two of them. She didn't need to add fuel to the fire.

Mace was just her best friend, nothing more—though certainly nothing less.

He was at her back as she walked through her office door and into the main room, the heat of him keeping her steady. The shop in Colorado Springs matched the one up north in layout, with only a few minor changes. Each station had its own cubicle area, but once people made it past the front section of the shop where onlookers couldn't peep in, it was almost all open. There were two private rooms in the back for those who wanted tattoos that required a little less clothing, as well as folding panels that could be placed in each of the artist's areas so they could be sectioned off easily. Most people didn't mind having other artists and clients watch them while they got a tattoo, and it usually added to the overall experience. As the licensed piercer in residence, Adrienne could do that part of her job in either of the rooms in the back, as well.

While some shops had closed-off rooms for each artist because the building was a converted home or office building, the Montgomerys hadn't wanted that. There was privacy when needed and socialization when desired. It was a great setup, and one Adrienne had been jealous of when she was working at her old place on the other side of the city.

"About time you made your way back here," Maya said dryly, her eyebrow ring glinting under the overhead light.

Adrienne flipped her cousin off then grinned as Maya did the same back. Of all her cousins, she and Maya looked the most alike. They each had long, dark hair, were average height, and had just the right amount of curves to make finding jeans difficult. Of course, Maya had birthed two kids, while Adrienne's butt came from her love of cookies…but that was neither here nor there.

Everyone stood around talking to one another, cups of water or coffee or tea in their hands as they looked around the place. As they weren't opening up for tattoos until later in the day, they were able to easily socialize in the main entry area. Their new hire, Ryan, stood off to the side, and Mace went over to him so they would be out of the way. They were really the only two non-Montgomerys, and she could only imagine how they felt.

"The location is pretty damn perfect," Shep said with a grin. His wife Shea stood by his side, their daughter Livvy bouncing between them. How her niece had gotten so big, Adrienne had no idea. Apparently, time flew when you had your head down, working. "We're the only tattoo shop around here, which will be good for business." They were located in a strip mall off the busiest road in their area—other than I-25, of course. That's how most of the businesses around were set up, with only the large market chains and restaurants having actual acreage behind them.

Adrienne nodded, though her stomach didn't quite agree. Most of the shops like hers were farther south, near the older parts of downtown. There were trendier places there, and a lot more people who looked like they did with ink and piercings. Up north, on North Academy Blvd, every building was the same: cream or tan-colored, and fit in almost like a bedroom community around the Air Force Academy.

Shep and Adrienne wanted not only the cadets but also everyone who lived in the sprawling neighborhood who wanted ink to find them and come back for more. Beginning something new was always difficult, but starting something new in an area of town that, from the outside at least, didn't look as if they'd fit in wouldn't make it any easier.

She knew that a lot of the prejudices about tattoo shops had faded away over time as the art became far more popular and almost normal, but she could still feel people's eyes on her when they noticed her ink.

"It's right next to a tea shop, a deli, a spice shop, Thea's bakery, and a few fancy shopping areas. I think you fit in nicely," Austin said, his arms folded over his chest as he looked around the place. "You almost have a little version of what we have up north. You just need a bookstore and a café where you can hang out."

"You're just spoiled because you don't even have to walk outside into the cold to get coffee or baked goods," Adrienne said dryly.

"That is true," Austin said with a laugh. "Adding in that side door that connects the two businesses was the best decision I ever made."

"I'll be sure to mention that to your wife," Shep said and ducked as Austin's arm shot out. The two men were nearly forty years old but fought like they were teens. Shea picked up Livvy and laughed before heading over to Maya. Adrienne didn't actually know her sister-in-law all that well since she hadn't seen her much, but now that the family had relocated, she knew that would change.

"They're going to break something," Thea said with a small laugh as she watched the two play-fight. She was the middle girl of the family but tended to act as if she were the eldest. When the retail spot three doors down from Thea's bakery had opened up, her sister had stopped at nothing to make sure Adrienne could move in. That was Thea, taking care of her family no matter what.

"Then they'll deserve it," Roxie, Adrienne's other sister said, shaking her head. "As long as they don't ruin something in the shop, of course," she added quickly after Adrienne shot her a look. "I meant break something on themselves." Roxie was the youngest of their immediate family, and often the quietest. None of them were truly quiet since they were Montgomerys, but Roxie sometimes fit the bill.

"Thanks for thinking of my shop that hasn't even had its first client yet." Adrienne wrapped her arm around Roxie's waist for a hug. "Where's Carter? I thought he said he'd be here."

Roxie and Carter had gotten married a few months ago, and Adrienne loved her brother-in-law, though she didn't know him all that well either. He worked long hours, and the couple tended to be very insular since they were still newlyweds.

Roxie's mouth twisted into a grimace before she schooled her features. "He couldn't get off work. He tried, but two guys called in, and he was up to his neck in carburetors."

Adrienne kissed her sister's temple and squeezed her tightly. "It's okay. It *is* the middle of the day, after all. I'm surprised any of you were able to take time off for this."

Tears formed at the backs of her eyes at the fact that

everyone *had* taken the time to be there for her and Shep. She blinked. She looked up from her sisters and tried not to let her emotions get to her, but then she met Mace's eyes. He gave her a curious look, and she smiled at him, trying to let him know that she was okay—just a little overwhelmed. Mace had a way of knowing what she felt without her saying it, and she didn't want him to worry. That's what happened when you were friends with someone as long as they had been.

"I just wish he would have come," Roxie said with a shrug. "It's fine. Everything is fine."

Adrienne met Thea's gaze, but the two sisters didn't say anything. If Roxie had something she wanted to share, she would. For now, everyone had other things on their minds. Namely, opening day.

Shep punched Austin in the shoulder one more time before backing away and grinning. "Okay, okay, I'm too old for this shit."

"True, you *are* too old." Austin winked, and Adrienne pinched the bridge of her nose.

"Great way to show everyone that we're all *so* professional and ready to lead with our own shop," she said, no bite to her tone. This was her family, and she was used to it all. If they weren't joking around and being loveable, adorable dorks, she'd have thought something was wrong.

"It's sort of what we signed on for," Ryan said with a wink. "Right, Mace? I mean, the legendary Montgomery antics are why *any* tattoo artist worth their salt wants to join up with them."

Mace gave them all a solemn nod, laughter dancing in his eyes. "It wouldn't be a Montgomery gathering without someone getting punched. Isn't that what you taught me, Adrienne?"

She flipped him off, knowing that Livvy's head was down so she wouldn't see. She tried not to be *too* bad of an influence on her niece.

"Okay, party people. Finish your drinks and cake and then let's clean up. We have three clients scheduled between one and two this afternoon, and Ryan is handling any walk-ins." Though she wasn't sure there would *be* any walk-ins since it was day one and they were doing a slow start. Some of their long-time clients had moved with them, and they already had a waiting list because of it, but that could change on a dime. Having word of mouth would be what made their shop a success, and that meant getting more clients in who weren't just the same ones from before.

The door opened, and she held back her frown. They weren't officially open yet, but it wasn't as if she could tell a potential customer off. The door *had* been unlocked, after all.

As a man in a nicely cut suit with a frown on his face walked in, Adrienne had a feeling this wouldn't be a client.

"Hi there, can I help you?" she asked, moving her way through the crowd. "We're opening in an hour or so, but if you need any information, I'm here."

The guy's face pinched, and she was worried that if he kept it up, it would freeze like that. "I'm not here for whatever it is this establishment does." His gaze traveled over her family's and friend's ink and clothing before it rested back on her. "I'm only here to tell you that you shouldn't finish unpacking."

"Excuse me?" Shep asked, his tone serious. The others stood back, letting Adrienne and Shep talk, but she knew they were all there if she needed them.

"You heard me." The man adjusted his tie. "I don't know how you got through the zoning board, but I can see they made a mistake. We don't want *your kind* here in our nice city. We're a growing community with families. Like I said, don't unpack. You won't be here long."

Before she could say anything in response to the ridiculous statement, the man turned on his heel and walked out of her building, leaving her family and friends standing beside her, all of them with shocked looks on their faces.

"Well, shit," Mace whispered then winced as he looked behind him to where Livvy was most likely with her mom.

"We'll figure out who that was. But, Adrienne, he won't be able to shut us down or whatever the hell he wants." Shep turned to her and gave her that big-brother stare. "Don't stress about him. He means nothing."

But she could tell from the look in his eyes, and the worried glances passing back and forth between her family members and friends that none of them quite believed that.

She had no idea who the man was, but she had a bad feeling about him. And every single warm feeling that had filled her at the sight of her family and friends coming together to celebrate the new shop fled, replaced by ice water in her veins.

So much for an easy opening day, she thought, and her stomach roiled again. Perhaps she would throw up because she just knew that wasn't the last time they'd see that man. Not by a long shot.

Find out more in FALLEN INK

To make sure you're up to date on all of Carrie Ann's releases, sign up for her mailing list HERE.

Delicate Ink

From New York Times Bestselling Author Carrie Ann Ryan's Montgomery Ink Series

DELICATE INK

On the wrong side of thirty, Austin Montgomery is ready to settle down. Unfortunately, his inked sleeves and scruffy beard isn't the suave business appearance some women crave. Only finding a woman who can deal with his job, as a tattoo artist and owner of Montgomery Ink, his seven meddling siblings, and his own gruff attitude won't be easy.

Finding a man is the last thing on Sierra Elder's mind. A recent transplant to Denver, her focus is on opening her own boutique. Wanting to cover up scars that run deeper than her flesh, she finds in Austin a man that truly gets to her—in more ways than one.

Although wary, they embark on a slow, tempestuous burn of a relationship. When blasts from both their pasts intrude on their present, however, it will take more than a promise of what could be to keep them together.

Find out more in Delicate Ink**. Out Now.**

To make sure you're up to date on all of Carrie Ann's releases, sign up for her mailing list HERE.

Love Restored

From New York Times Bestselling Author Carrie Ann Ryan's Gallagher Brothers series

Love Restored

In the first of a Montgomery Ink spin-off series from NYT Bestselling Author Carrie Ann Ryan, a broken man uncovers the truth of what it means to take a second chance with the most unexpected woman…

Graham Gallagher has seen it all. And when tragedy struck, lost it all. He's been the backbone of his brothers, the one they all rely on in their lives and business. And when it comes to falling in love and creating a life, he knows what it's like to have it all and watch it crumble. He's done with looking for another person to warm his bed, but apparently he didn't learn his lesson because the new piercer at Montgomery Ink tempts him like no other.

Blake Brennen may have been born a trust fund baby, but

she's created a whole new life for herself in the world of ink, piercings, and freedom. Only the ties she'd thought she'd cut long ago aren't as severed as she'd believed. When she finds Graham constantly in her path, she knows from first glance that he's the wrong kind of guy for her. Except that Blake excels at making the wrong choice and Graham might be the ultimate temptation for the bad girl she'd thought long buried.

Find out more in Love Restored**. Out Now.**

To make sure you're up to date on all of Carrie Ann's releases, sign up for her mailing list HERE.

CPSIA information can be obtained
at www.ICGtesting.com
Printed in the USA
LVHW05s1927290518
578848LV00012B/1354/P